"IT'S THE CAT'S PAJAMAS."
—*Tulsa World*

*More praise for Lydia Adamson's
Alice Nestleton Mysteries . . .*

"Witty . . . slyly captivating."   —*Publishers Weekly*

"A plucky heroine."   —*Library Journal*

"A blend of the sublime with a tinge of suspense as Alice, like her four-pawed friends, uses her uncanny intuition to solve a baffling mystery."
          —*Mystery Reviews*

"Whimsical. Lifts readers out of the doldrums with cheery characters who steal the show."
          —*Midwest Book Review*

"An ideal stocking stuffer for cat-doting mystery fans."   —*Roanoke Times*

"Cleverly written, suspenseful . . . the perfect gift for the cat lover."   —*Lake Worth Herald*

Other books in the Alice Nestleton mystery series

A CAT ON JINGLE BELL ROCK

An Alice Nestleton Mystery

Lydia Adamson

A SIGNET BOOK

SIGNET
Published by the Penguin Group
Penguin Putnam Inc., 375 Hudson Street,
New York, New York 10014, U.S.A.
Penguin Books Ltd, 27 Wrights Lane,
London W8 5TZ, England
Penguin Books Australia Ltd,
Ringwood, Victoria, Australia
Penguin Books Canada Ltd, 10 Alcorn Avenue,
Toronto, Ontario, Canada M4V 3B2
Penguin Books (N.Z.) Ltd, 182–190 Wairau Road,
Auckland 10, New Zealand

Penguin Books Ltd, Registered Offices:
Harmondsworth, Middlesex, England

Published by Signet, an imprint of Dutton NAL,
a member of Penguin Putnam Inc.
Previously appeared in a Dutton edition.

First Signet Printing, October, 1998
10 9 8 7 6 5 4 3 2 1

Chapter 1

The snow came on December 7. At just a bit past seven in the evening.

I was entranced by the dropping flakes—thick, silent, mysterious, seemingly without end.

Oh, my! I thought. It's like being a child again in Minnesota. Like watching my grandmother's farm get covered by a white blanket: the yard, the fields, the house, the dairy barn, the car, the truck. Everything white.

I scooped my cats up, Bushy in my right arm, Pancho in my left.

We stood by the huge loft window framing the Manhattan night.

"Look, you foolish things!" I said to the two of them. "How can you be so blasé? That's real snow. And if you misbehave, I shall dump you in it. Understand?"

They yawned at my threats, but they did finally stare out at the falling flakes. Then I kissed each of my beasts on the nose and I let them down.

I was feeling quite good. Only seventeen days to Christmas. And this year I was going to get a tree. Let the cats chew on it as much as they wanted. I definitely was going to get a tree. But it was much too early. Prices were too high. I knew I would end up buying the tree only when the sidewalk vendors started discounting them wildly, forty-eight hours before Christmas Day. And I wouldn't shop for presents until the twenty-fourth. I just decided to let chaos and anarchy rule my Christmas holiday this year.

Yes, I was feeling quite good. Even though I hadn't been called for any acting work in almost six months. Even though my cat-sitting business seemed moribund. Even though I wasn't getting along any too well with my once and future lover—Anthony "Mr. Stage Design" Basillio. And even though my net worth was $131.61.

I went to brew myself a cup of hard-core peppermint tea.

Then the phone rang. I was sure it was Tony calling.

It wasn't.

A gruff voice boomed loudly into my ear: "Is this the actress Alice Nestleton? The one who did *Trojan Women* in '86—at the Public?"

Well, I thought, whoever this nutcase is, at least he knows one of the productions in which, if you'll pardon my bragging, I distinguished myself.

"Yes," I said, after a rather long interval during which the caller wheezed and cleared his throat repeatedly, "I am that Alice Nestleton."

"Great. Alice, this is Jack Rugow. How the hell are you?"

I was dumbstruck. Jack Rugow? I hadn't spoken to him in a good five years. He was the producer, director, general manager, and chief bottle washer of the last remaining legitimate repertory company in Manhattan. It was called simply the Rep, and it did four plays a year: one Shakespeare, one American classic (usually O'Neill), one European comedy, and always one first play by an unknown. Everything about the Rep was top-drawer, and roly-poly Jack Rugow was the reason.

He did not give me time to make small talk. "I

know this is short notice," he said. "And it's snowing like crazy. But I'm at a bar on Jane Street called the Corner Bistro, and I want to buy you a drink."

"Now?"

"Now!"

All I said, visions of a juicy part dancing in my head, was "Twenty minutes."

I was there in fifteen. The bar was not the usual jumble of locals and college students and office workers. The floor was tracked with slush from dripping boots. I shook my snow hat off and looked for Jack.

He wasn't at the bar up front. He was sitting in a booth at the back, playing with the ketchup bottle.

Then he saw me and waved wildly. I slid into the seat across from him. Bless him. He was wearing an old-fashioned snowflake and bobsled–motif sweater.

"You look wonderful, Alice!" he said cheerily.

"Well, thank you."

"What do you want to drink?"

"Nothing, thank you."

"No? Well, I'm going to say yes to life even if you won't." He walked to the bar and came back with a bourbon, straight up, in one hand and a glass of water in the other.

I studied his face. He seemed to have calmed down a bit since last we met, to be a little less manic. His hair was still combed straight back, and he still wore his clothing as if he were a rakish Brando manqué. He wasn't, though. He didn't act at all.

"It's not supposed to snow until Christmas," Jack said. Then he reached across the table, grabbed my hand, and said, "Thanks for meeting me like this. You always were a trouper, Alice."

Then he released my hand, leaned back, and said rather gravely, "I want to talk to you about sustenance."

I felt those pangs of hope and desire.

A part! Yes! This man is about to offer me a role in a new play called *Sustenance*.

"It's a nice title," I said casually. "Who wrote it?"

"Wrote what?"

"*Sustenance* . . . the play."

"No, dear. Sustenance isn't a play. It's a place. Sustenance House. It's a charity. You know, they feed the poor and shelter the homeless, run a thrift shop. Things like that. Haven't you ever heard of it?"

"No."

"It's famous for the goose dinners for the homeless on Christmas Day. Seven hundred dinners served with all the trimmings. Can you imagine that?"

I repeated, "No."

My blood was beginning to boil. Was it possible that he had lured me out in the snow just to hit me up for a donation to his pet charity? Me, with a hundred thirty-one bucks in the bank.

He seemed lost in thought. I got even madder. I had the urge to crown him with that ketchup bottle.

But then he asked, very quietly, "Are the rumors about you true?"

"What rumors?" I asked, eyes wide.

"That you have a very 'interesting' hobby."

"Like what?"

"Well, not model trains. I mean an interest in things . . . criminal."

"Are you in trouble, Jack?"

"No. Not me personally. But Sustenance House is. And we need help desperately, Alice."

"What is your connection with this place?"

"I'm on the board of directors. When I'm not at the Rep, I'm there. It's a big part of my life now.

Can you understand? I want to do more than entertain people. I want to help them."

"Yes, Jack, of course I can understand wanting to help people." Suddenly all my anger at him was gone.

"Let me explain something," he said, pain in his voice. "We need your help now—immediately. Here's the story: Around this time every year we get an extremely generous anonymous donation—$81,000, to be exact. It's a pretty impressive figure, isn't it?"

"Indeed it is."

"For twelve years, like clockwork, we've received that amount. We use it for our now-famous Christmas feeding, but also to make the following year's mortgage payments on the old building, help people out with emergency medical bills, and so on."

He turned his palms up before continuing. "But this year . . . no gift. No $81,000."

"Why?"

"We don't know. In fact it may have been donated as usual, but we simply didn't receive it."

Jack finished off his whiskey.

"It sounds crazy, doesn't it, Alice? Well, it *is*

crazy. The money is mailed to us by regular first-class mail. Our anonymous donor doesn't even register or certify the package. Worse, he or she doesn't send a check. The money comes in postal and bank money orders. A big stack of each, because the post office has a limit of $700 per money order and banks have a $1,000 limit.

"Of course, the donor could get a single certified bank check for the entire amount, but then his name would have to appear on the check. Anyway, we figure one of three things might have happened. One, he might just have decided to stop making the donation. Right?"

"Sure," I said.

"Or two, the person might have died. Right?"

"Right."

"Or three, it's simply that after twelve years our luck has run out and the package was lost in the mail."

"Does he make the money orders out to Sustenance House before he mails the package?"

"No. All blanks. No payer listed. No payee. Just blanks. The director deposits them as cash after endorsing them."

"How can I help you, Jack?"

"We have to find the anonymous donor. If he

or she is alive and has just stopped supporting us, well, fine. But if the package was taken or lost in the mail, maybe he'll help out this time and learn not to act so foolishly in the future. We've spoken to the police. They can't help. 'Where's the crime?' they said. It doesn't even fit in the missing person category. Someone suggested putting ads in the papers. But what's the point of that? Our donor doesn't want to be found."

He made another trip to the bar and returned with two more bourbons, one for me, I imagined. But I didn't drink it.

"Listen, Alice. There's a board of directors' meeting tonight at Sustenance House."

"In this weather?"

"Yes. Everyone will be a bit late, but so what? I told the executive director of Sustenance about you. He encouraged me to talk to you. Come with me to the meeting? You'll like him, really. David Devries is a fascinating character. He was a war hero, a pilot in Vietnam. Then he became an advertising big shot. Then he got faith and joined the Christian Brothers. When he lost faith, he joined the brotherhood of the bottle and ended up in the gutter. When he got sober, he started Sustenance House."

Jack downed his second drink, then emptied the glass of water in a single gulp. He signaled that he was finished with his repast. He waited for my answer like a roly-poly leopard ready to pounce.

But I hesitated.

"We can get a cab," he said.

"No cabs available in this snow," I replied.

"I'll get one," he promised.

So I agreed. He was as good as his word. He did get a taxi. But it took us an hour to crawl uptown to the four-story building on a dingy block between First and Second avenues, just under an exit ramp for the Fifty-ninth Street bridge.

It looked like an ordinary dwelling until you walked inside, and then you immediately perceived it to be some kind of institutional facility. There were classrooms and cafeterias and meeting rooms and bulletin boards—and some very strange-looking people drifting around the corridors.

"We only put up seventeen homeless people a night, but we feed more than a hundred right here, and we deliver at least that many meals each night," Jack said proudly.

He used a key to open the door to a room. "Look here, Alice. A stage! Did you think I would let them get away without a theater on the premises?" He laughed heartily.

I stared inside. The stage was very small. "It's nice, Jack. What kinds of things do you put on?"

"To date, nothing."

We then took a tiny, slow-moving elevator up to the fourth floor. "We're on our way to the posh sanctum of the executive offices," he said mockingly. "Don't you love our high-speed elevator?"

The doors opened on a meeting room. There was a long, plain table with folding chairs placed around it, a blackboard on a stand, several file cabinets, and a bookcase.

We sat right down. I noticed the little puddle on the floor and realized that I had forgotten to take my boots off.

Behind us a door slammed, and a tall, stooped, painfully thin man in shabby clothing glided in and sat at the head of the table. His head was shaved, and he looked haunted but kind. No, almost saintly.

Jack introduced me to David Devries.

"I am happy you came this evening," the

executive director said, "and so very grateful that you will be helping us."

He began to sort through the papers in the folder on the table.

The rest of the board began to arrive. One after another they came out of the elevator, in five-minute intervals, shedding their snowy garments along the way.

Jack whispered a brief identification in my ear for each: Samuel Mortimer, hospital administrator; Raya Lambert, hat designer; Will Holland, travel writer; Ishmael Rood, restaurateur.

There were nods all around, but no words spoken. Each director sat down and began to pull out pads, papers, writing implements.

David Devries called the meeting to order with a clearing of his throat. "As you can see," he began, "we have a visitor. Her name is Alice Nestleton, and she is a good friend of Jack's. I will explain the reason for her presence after the meeting."

The hat designer smiled warmly at me.

Another person entered from the back. She had disheveled straw-colored hair. She pulled out a chair and sat down just behind Devries.

"Our stenographer," Jack explained to me under his breath. "Daisy Eidan. Former homeless lady. Darvon addict. She lives here. Takes the minutes."

Devries stared at his elegant-looking fountain pen, tapped it once lightly on the desk, and said, "What we need right now are some ideas about obtaining quick, short-term funding. Christmas is just seventeen days away."

He had a clipped, patrician New England accent, almost British. There was something harsh about him, ascetic, that elicited attention and . . . well, deference.

Samuel Mortimer, who was wearing a well-cut Italian suit, asked, "Can you give us a dollar-and-cents figure? I mean, what is needed right now?"

Before Devries could respond, the travel writer, Will Holland, burst out laughing.

Startled, everyone stared at him.

He bent over, opened his briefcase, thrust his hand in, and pulled out several objects, which he flung onto the table. They were small candy canes, each wrapped in clear cellophane.

"I thought we should open the meeting with a little snack," he announced, sliding a piece of candy toward each person at the table.

No one made a move to pick up the candy.

"Is he drunk?" Jack asked Devries worriedly.

"I think it may be a bit too early for the Christmas party," Devries said firmly, as if he had had long experience dealing with cases of temporary derangement.

Holland laughed again, sounding deranged indeed. "Oh, no! It's never too early for a Christmas party, my friends," he crowed. "But if you don't like candy canes, I have something else for you."

He reached once again into his briefcase and this time pulled out a number of small water pistols and dumped them onto the table in the same manner as he'd dumped the candy.

"They're all loaded . . . ready to squirt," he yelled, and began distributing the toys to each director.

Again those present sat frozen, not touching the objects.

"What's the matter? You don't believe they work?" asked Holland.

He then picked up the one in front of him, pressed it to his temple, and pulled the trigger.

The bullet that entered his skull sent him and his metal chair toppling over.

I distinctly remember that I refused for the longest time to look at the dead man on the floor.

No, instead I kept staring at the candy cane and water pistol on the table in front of me.

Chapter 2

The following day—fifteen hours after the tragedy—the board of directors of Sustenance House met again.

Same place. Same cast. Except for Will Holland, of course.

We all were still dazed. We looked nervously at one another, and then our eyes quickly scanned the tabletop for unwanted objects. There were none.

I didn't want to be there, but my conscience demanded it. And consciences, around Christmastime, tend to exhibit unaccustomed powers.

The executive director dealt with the tragedy quickly, compassionately, and expertly. "I was at the precinct until two in the morning. I'll tell you all I learned. The detectives contacted and interviewed a writing associate of Will Holland's, someone who knew him a lot better than we knew him. It seems that Will has been deeply depressed during the past three years, since the death of his younger brother. He has been on and off a number of medications during that time, and this constant shifting of antidepressants made him spin out of control often.

"Anyway, that is what I was told, and I am relaying it to you as I heard it. I have sent condolences to his family from all of us at Sustenance House. The funeral will be private."

There was a long silence. Then Samuel Mortimer said, "It's strange. I never thought of him as depressed, merely as thoughtful."

Raya Lambert said, "What I can't get over are the water pistols. The whole ritual was so bizarre. And believe me, I thought the gun he picked up was also a water pistol."

Devries nodded.

"I saw the weapon again at the precinct. It does look like a water pistol. But it's a little more deadly, obviously. One of the detectives told me it's a French-made .25 caliber—very rarely seen in the U.S."

Jack Rugow was drumming his fingers nervously on the table. When Devries finished, Jack looked at Raya, nodding up and down.

"You know what you just said? About a ritual? That's exactly right. I called a shrink friend yesterday after it happened. He said that many suicides perform some kind of ritual before they do it. The trouble is, the ritual has meaning only for them. Like taking all the coins out of their pocket and stacking them. Or building a house of cards. Or taking all their socks out of a drawer and carefully folding them. With Will, it was the candy canes and water pistols. Sort of like a Japanese No drama. You know what I mean?"

This theoretical discourse on the relationship between presuicide rituals and one aspect of Asian theater was cut short by an impatient Devries.

"Let's get to Miss Nestleton now," he said. I squirmed. Then he signaled to the stenographer, Daisy, that what followed would be off the record. Daisy, her hair still wildly disheveled, accepted the judgment stoically. I realized, with chagrin, that I hadn't even noticed she was in the room again. Then I realized that she was, upon reflection, much younger than she looked at first.

What the hell is a recovering Darvon addict supposed to look like? And why Darvon?

Devries said, "I want to tell you who Miss Nestleton is and why she was invited here. She is a friend of Jack's. She is a very fine actress on the New York stage. But she is, most important for our purposes, a woman who has a unique talent in solving certain kinds of problems, usually criminal ones. She has agreed to make an attempt to identify and locate our suddenly vanished patron. I want her to know that we all will help her in any way possible."

Raya laughed and pointed out: "We'd love to help Miss Nestleton. But we know nothing about him . . . or her, as the case may be. Absolutely nothing."

"Not *absolutely* nothing," Devries corrected her. He motioned to the stenographer, who rose, disappeared into the back, and returned with an attaché case.

Devries took the case, placed it on the table, and snapped open the lid.

"For some reason," he said, "I saved all the outer packaging of the money orders. For all twelve years."

Then he looked at me and smiled wanly. "Here

it is, Miss Nestleton. It isn't much, but it's all we have."

He removed a stack of small manila envelopes held together with a rubber band.

"These were the outside mailers. Same every year. All twelve of them."

He placed the envelopes back into the attaché case and pulled out another packet.

"Inside each mailer," he explained, "were stacks of money orders, as you know. And each stack was wrapped in a New York City bus map. Here are the maps—some thirty of them."

He held them up for a moment. Jack Rugow groaned. Devries placed them back into the case.

Finally he removed a very small packet consisting of pieces of paper held together with a paper clip.

"And here are the notes he enclosed with each mailing. One-line cryptic little messages. I didn't know what they meant when I received them, and I don't know now." He smiled at me. "That's why Miss Nestleton is here. If anyone will know, she will."

He returned the packet of notes to the attaché case, slammed the lid with a flourish, and pushed it across the table to me.

Everyone in the room turned eyes on me. I realized they were waiting for some kind of exuberant response. I gave Jack Rugow a quick and dirty look. Were these people in their right minds? Did they really expect me to locate this missing Andrew Carnegie with a few packets of anonymous junk like this?

I stared at the wall. It occurred to me for the first time that while the whole of Sustenance House had already been decorated for Christmas—a riotous mélange of homeless-made wreaths and drawings and crazy-looking stockings—the meeting room had only one decoration on the wall. It was a large black silhouette of Santa and his reindeer. Donner. Blitzen. Prancer. Dancer . . . uh . . . I tried to remember the rest of the reindeer. I couldn't. I turned to David Devries and gave him one of my best fake smiles.

"I'll do my best," I said.

"Now let's get down to some serious fundraising," Devries said to his board. I picked up my new attaché case, bade adieu to Santa and his reindeer, and took the elevator down.

A few hours later I was seated in my friend Nora's tiny office in the back of her theater district bistro, Pal Joey. Nora sat behind her hopelessly cluttered desk. She was taking a breather between lunch and dinner traffic. As usual, she was exhausted. After all, she was the hostess, maître d', half-time chef, even, in a pinch, waitress. In fact there wasn't one aspect of the operation that she wasn't perpetually butting into, even though it ran quite smoothly without her. Pal Joey was a success. The location was perfect. The food was quite good—almost spectacular, in fact, when Nora was doing the cooking. The bar was homey. The restaurant dim enough for trysts, happy enough for families, and "Broadway" enough for theatergoers and performers alike.

"You look like a diplomat with that attaché case," Nora said. "Don't you know actresses don't carry those kinds of things? It's gauche, Al."

"Tony will be here in a few minutes," I answered.

"He will? Why? Something going on?"

"Let's wait till he gets here. I'll tell you then. But first, would it be possible for me to clear your desk?"

She looked as if I had hit her with a cold towel.

But a minute later she was laughing. "Alice," she said, "I've never seen the surface of this desk since I opened the place. I don't *want* to see it. I think it's probably bad luck to clear all this stuff away. Like when I was an understudy for Gwen Verdon once. Did I ever tell you about that? She got the flu, and it actually looked as if I was going to go on—on Broadway, mind you. You know how seldom something like that happens. So there I was, ready to leap into stardom. And then I slipped on the floor of the rehearsal studio and sprained my ankle so bad I couldn't even stand up, much less dance."

"So? What does this have to do with clearing off your desk?"

"Wood, Alice. Wood surface! I don't do well with wood surfaces, and underneath all this clutter is a vintage 1925 wooden secretary."

"Nora, you're being ridiculous."

Before her horrified eyes I proceeded to remove everything and neatly pile it in one of the ubiquitous cardboard boxes she employed as file cabinets. Most of them had once held ketchup bottles.

When the desk was bare, I laid the closed attaché case on it.

"It looks menacing, Alice. Is there a bomb in it?"

"No. How do you like the top of your desk?"

Nora ran her hand over the smooth surface. "Actually it feels pretty nice," she admitted.

Then Tony arrived. He was wearing a longshoreman's wool cap and a pea coat.

"It stopped snowing, and it's turning hellish cold," he said. Then he kissed me, whispering, "Cold weather turns me on."

"What doesn't?" I said. I laughed and pushed him away, then commanded, "Sit down, Tony."

He whipped off his hat and sat down quickly, as if obeying a severe schoolmarm. He didn't know that I was having very unschoolmarmish thoughts just then. My, how handsome he is, I was thinking. The cold weather suits him, gives his face a wonderful rosy cast. And his black hair is gorgeous now, speckled with gray and all tousled from his cap.

"I just got a letter from my ex-wife, complaining about my child support payments. She called me a degenerate."

"You don't look like a degenerate, Tony," Nora commented. "You look like a middle-aged man who once played a revival of *On the Waterfront* in New Britain, Connecticut."

"Let's get down to business," I said, trying to nip Nora's flight of fancy in the bud.

"Wait just a minute," she answered sassily, and rushed out of the office only to return a minute later with three glasses and a bottle of red wine. "Now that my desk is finally clear," she said, "we might as well use it for something." She poured a little wine into each glass.

Then I proceeded to tell her and Basillio what had transpired during the last twenty-four hours, what was in the attaché case, what the Sustenance House directors hoped I would accomplish.

When I finished, there was a long silence.

Finally Tony said, "They must be kidding."

I said, "Since what I am now investigating is a sort of postal crime, I thought it would be better to gather together. I mean, after all, who knows more about mailing things than New York theater people—right? Résumés. Photos. You name it. We keep the postal system alive."

"Actually," said Nora in an offhand fashion, "it was a brilliant idea to call me and Tony in on this. See, I have it solved without even looking into that attaché case."

"What are you talking about?"

"Alice, if this person was crazy enough to mail unregistered and noncertified blank money orders for $81,000 every year, he was obviously operating from a mental institution. Or is in one now. That narrows the search considerably, wouldn't you say?"

I ignored her brilliant analysis and removed the outside mailers first.

We all got up from our chairs and hovered over the twelve envelopes. Each one was addressed in the exact same manner: large printed script by a black Magic Marker.

"To: Executive Director—Sustenance House"

Then the address and zip code.

No return address whatsoever.

On the bottom left hand of each envelope was written, in the same hand that had written the address: "First Class."

"Well," Tony said, "at least we know one thing about the man—if he's a man."

"What's that?" Nora asked.

"That he doesn't have any patience," he said.

"How do you come to that conclusion?" I asked.

"He didn't want to wait on any lines. He never took the packages to a teller's window. If you take an envelope to a window in the post office to mail it, the clerk weighs it, right? And then puts an adhesive strip on the package with the amount required. Then they use a first-class rubber stamp usually. But this guy weighed the envelope himself, then went to the machine, bought a whole batch of different kinds of stamps, and put about a buck too much postage on each envelope ... just to be sure."

It was an inspired deduction. I studied the envelope, festooned with many, many kinds of stamps in differing denominations.

"Wait a minute, Tony," Nora objected. "He had to go to the clerk to get money orders. Alice said the payments were made half in bank money orders and half in postal money orders. So why stand on line for a money order and then not have the clerk weigh and send the package at the same time?"

"Because," Tony explained, his voice rising just a bit in excitement, "they often ask you to put a return address on a package if you haven't already done it. And that is something our friend could not abide."

Oh, dear! Tony was on fire.

He began moving the envelopes around, rearranging them on the desk.

"What are you doing?" I asked.

He held up his hand for quiet, like a conductor.

Then he grinned. "And I'll tell you something even stranger."

"What?"

"He mailed twelve envelopes in twelve years—right?"

"Right."

"Well, he mailed each one from a different zip code. Look at the postmarks."

It was astonishing. Nora and I bent over the desk intently. Tony was right.

"Give me a piece of paper," I demanded.

Nora ripped out a sheet from an old calendar and handed me her ballpoint pen, the one I knew she reserved for check signing.

I wrote down the zip code from which the first envelope was mailed, twelve years ago: 10029.

The next year, 10128. And the next 10028.

Then 10021. Then 10044. Then, successively: 10022, 10017, 10016, 10010, 10009, 10002.

And the one from last year—back to 10029.

"Why did he do that?" Nora asked.

"Probably he thought it safer to buy his money orders in a different post office each year," Tony said.

She nodded in agreement. "And he probably

did the same with his bank money orders. An extra-careful individual."

I was listening to what they said with only one ear. Something else was bothering me.

"I need the yellow pages," I said to Nora. She dug out the Manhattan directory and plopped it onto the desk. I turned to the back page, which contains the zip code map of Manhattan Island.

I placed my list next to the map.

We all saw what our anonymous donor had done.

"I can't believe it," Tony said.

"Believe it!" I said. "He mailed the first package from around 110th Street—*East* 110th Street. The next one from the zip code just south of that, also on the East Side . . . and then in subsequent years he worked his way down through every zip code on the East Side of Manhattan—from Spanish Harlem to the southernmost tip of Manhattan Island."

"But why?" asked Nora.

"I have no idea—except I assume that he was trying to be 'careful.' Notice, he began and ended in zip code 10029. There are only eleven codes on the East Side of Manhattan south of 116th Street. He ran out of codes, so last year he returned to the first one he'd ever used, the one I'm guessing was his own zip, in his own neighborhood—10029."

I paused and tapped the map gleefully. "So our hero either lives between 97th and 116th streets on the East Side and each year traveled a bit farther downtown. *Or* he moved every year—moved farther downtown, that is—which seems highly unlikely. This means that we now know where he lives."

"What a breakthrough," Nora remarked sardonically. "That narrows the field to about half a million people."

"Well, it's a start," Tony noted, sounding skeptical.

"And now for the bus maps," I said, pushing the phone book and envelopes aside.

I placed on the desk the bus maps that the philanthropist had used to wrap the money orders in and then placed in the mailing envelopes.

Tony picked up one map, unfolded it completely, and then held it high above his head. "At least," he said, "our friend acts rationally in some areas."

"What do you mean? What's rational about using bus maps?" asked Nora. "Or irrational, for that matter?"

"Since they're printed on both sides, on glossy paper, even if you hold the envelope up to the light, you can't see what's inside it. It's like your aunt Ethel sending you a five-dollar bill for your birthday. You wrap cash in several sheets of paper—or a birthday card or something—so nobody sees it through the envelope. Well, a blank money order's the same as cash."

"Good point, Tony. But the maps alone tell us nothing," I interjected. "Maybe he made some kind of notation on one of them—tracing a route or something like that."

We examined the maps carefully. There wasn't a single mark on any of them.

"Maybe the guy just liked riding buses," Nora said, shrugging. "Maybe he took buses from one neighborhood to another, one zip code to the next. And there's nothing on the maps because if he lives where we think he lives, you don't need a map to travel straight downtown on the East Side. It's the easiest thing in the world. You travel straight down Second Avenue. That's a very simple, direct bus route."

"Or," Tony added, "the York Avenue bus. He could take that downtown."

"But that doesn't go all the way downtown," she objected. "It turns west at Fifty-seventh Street."

"So? Let him transfer at—"

I stepped in. "Hold it, hold it! Let's not get into a fight over bus routes." I realized that without any markings the maps were probably worthless to us anyway.

I gathered the maps together, refastened them with the rubber band. Then I brought out the heavy ammunition: the twelve little slips of paper.

"Our mystery patron included a short note in each packet. It accompanied the money. Here are all twelve of them—one for every year he made the donation. The first one reads: *Feed Them*."

"Makes sense," Tony conceded.

"The second one," I went on, "says, *Remember Them*."

At that point I spread the notes out so that the others could see them. The notes all were in the same childlike script as the handwriting on the front of each manila envelope.

Tony read the other ten slips aloud: "Third one: *Assist Them*. Fourth: *Nurture Them*. Fifth: *Keep Them*.

Sixth: *Love Them.* Seventh: *Oblige Them.* Eighth: *Enlighten Them.* Ninth: *Befriend Them.* Tenth: *Favor Them.* Eleventh: *Receive Them.* Twelfth: *Attend Them.*

"And that's it. The twelve pillars of wisdom," Tony concluded.

"Hmm. The Sermon on the Mount, it ain't," Nora said. "But there is something kind of nice about his little comments. I think he was just reminding them that the money he was sending was for the poor and the wretched—not for executive salaries or PR campaigns. And that makes sense."

I kept reading the notes over and over. I needed them to make a different kind of sense, to reveal something. But they would not yield. They just lay there—pathetic, childish, imperative sentences. Commands. Pleas.

Nora poured more wine in all our glasses. "I think it's time we packed it in, Alice. They didn't give you enough to go on. In fact they didn't give you anything, really. There is just no way you're going to find him on the basis of those scraps of paper and bus information."

"*Him or her,*" put in Tony. "We haven't ruled out the possibility the donor is a woman."

"I have," said Nora calmly.

"Have you, Nora?" I asked. "Based on what?"

"Based on the fact that I'll eat my appointment book if this wacko isn't a man. No woman would behave that way. It's dumb. I mean, a rich woman would just have her lawyer take care of it if she didn't want this charity to know where the checks came from. Can you imagine having that much dough to spend at Christmas and wasting your time with all these meshugah mail drops and money orders and mystery notes? No! Never in a million years. A woman would be out shopping to beat the band. Wouldn't you?"

"Good question, Nora. But for now I think we should keep at it."

"At what? It's a dead end, Alice!" she exploded.

"She's right," said Tony. "You're spinning your wheels, Swede."

I sat down and took a long drink of wine.

"I have work to do around here," Nora said impatiently.

"And I'm starving," Tony stated.

"But I am thinking of the Unabomber," I said somberly.

Nora hit the roof again. "The Unabomber! What does that idiot have to do with this donor? The Unabomber is a criminal. He murdered people.

The person you're looking for is a good guy. One of the very good guys."

"Nora has a point," Tony noted.

At last here was something the two of them agreed on. Usually they fought like a couple of alley cats. "Just hear me out," I said. "The Unabomber sent his murderous devices through the U.S. mail for some twenty years. He was never caught, never traced. But then his craving to be 'appreciated' finally overwhelmed him. And he had to have his manifesto published in the *Times* and the *Washington Post*. That's what did him in. The document was recognized by his estranged brother. End of case."

"Hold on a minute, Alice," Nora said, disbelief in her voice. "You're not—you can't be saying that the *New York Times* is going to publish those scraps of paper! Those twelve crazy notes with the sayings on them."

She didn't give me time to answer. She was like a runaway train. "Even if they do publish them," she said, "so what? You simply can't tell anything from them. A ten-year-old kid could write, 'Feed Them.' So could an eighty-year-old. The Unabomber wrote a thirty-thousand-word manifesto."

"Take it easy, Nora. All I'm saying is that it's

odd for such a secretive, an obsessively secretive man like our philanthropist to enclose notes of any kind. Never mind how profound or how silly they are. I think it must mean something that he wrote those notes."

I was met with a stony, skeptical silence.

"Well," I said, "let me fiddle with this a bit more. You two go about your business."

Nora walked out of the room without another word. Tony bent down, kissed my neck, and said quietly, "Nero fiddled, and look what happened to him."

Then he rushed out to catch up with Nora. It is amazing how easily the prospect of a good hamburger can turn a grown man into a desperate, groveling creature.

I was alone with the evidence, if you could call it that: the manila envelopes, the bus maps, and, before me, the twelve messages of Christmas charity.

I began to recite them: *Feed Them, Remember Them, Assist Them, Nurture Them,* and so on. But I soon grew weary and laid my head on the desk.

Oh, this whole episode was becoming tiring. Whatever had led me to believe I could help Sustenance House? But I had to give it a try, didn't

I? Did I have any choice? Faith, hope, and charity, and the last is the most important. Charity; *Caritas*—it means love.

Too bad for Sustenance House. And too bad for all the homeless people it helped. It seemed that only the geese would be happy with my failure.

To quote Count Basie, "one more time." Go over the notes one more time, I instructed myself. And I did, reading them slowly, looking minutely at the script of each one.

A ten-year-old kid could have written them. That's what Nora had said. Nora was right. The notes were oddly childish in both execution of penmanship and in their naive terseness.

Now where would a child get eighty-one thousand dollars to send each year? That child was getting a very generous allowance.

No, I thought, after I had worried that bone a bit, there is no way it could be a child. Perhaps a devout sort of person who took seriously "Except ye be as little children, ye will not enter the kingdom. . . ."

I tried to think what I would do, in a childlike fashion, both to hide and to reveal.

Some kind of giggling-adolescent code, the kind kids always construct with their friends to keep secrets. Like my playmate Gloria, who used to answer sweetly, "Yes," to everything, and then whisper the number 29, which was the sum of the numerical equivalents of *N* (14) and *O* (15). But those kinds of codes never go from letters to numbers; it is always the other way around.

Besides, there weren't enough words to make it some kind of translation code . . . from one thing to another.

What about an acronym? I thought. That made sense. Not much but some. I had the sinking feeling that this whole train of thought was going nowhere fast. But I had to do something.

I lined the slips up again, this time carefully, in a single row. From the first sent to the last.

I walked my fingers through the slips.

Feed Them
Remember Them
Assist Them
Nurture Them
Keep Them
Love Them
Oblige Them
Enlighten Them

What I suddenly saw hit me with such force I could not believe it. I shook my head and began to laugh a bit nervously.

I leaned far back, stretched, and then leaned forward into the fray again.

No, I wasn't fantasizing. I wasn't hallucinating. The answer was there—plain as Laurence Olivier naked in your shower.

The first letter of the first word in each of the first five notes spelled out FRANK. The first letter of the first word in each of the next four notes spelled out LOEB. Frank Loeb. Frank Loeb. Frank Loeb. I repeated the name again and again.

Then I got up slowly, went to the door of the office, opened it, and called out for Tony and Nora. They didn't seem to heed my call. So then I screamed, and they came running.

"I need the white pages. I need the white pages," I babbled.

"First the yellow pages, now the white. Why not have a nice hamburger, Alice? What's the matter?"

"We know him. We know his name, Nora!"

Nora handed me the phone book, and I began flipping through the pages like a madwoman.

Yes! There was one Frank Loeb in the Manhattan white pages. What's more, he lived in the exact neighborhood we had predicted: the 10029 zip code. His address was on East Ninety-eighth Street between First and Second avenues.

Tony said, "We all knew you were beautiful, Swede, and we all know you can act. But whoever figured you were smart?"

I gave Tony three hours to do what he had to do. I went home and fed my cats.

At exactly nine in the evening we met at the corner of First Avenue and Twenty-third Street. It had got a bit warmer and was starting to snow lightly again, but this time the flakes were small and, well, kind of ugly.

We boarded the First Avenue bus going north. There were very few people on it. Tony, of course, did not have a token, so I provided.

"What are we going to do when we see him?" he asked.

"I'll worry about that when I see him."

"Why don't you just tell the people at Sustenance House and let them take it from there? They're not paying you for this."

"The acronym could be a coincidence," I replied.

"You know, that occurred to me too," Tony replied with a laugh. "But I didn't want to irritate you."

We got off the bus at Ninety-sixth Street and found the address quickly.

It was a badly run-down five-story dwelling.

Tony was staring at the apartment house in absolute puzzlement. "Why would a guy who can afford an $81,000 charitable donation for the homeless live in a dump like this?"

A Hispanic man and two young boys were shoveling the front of the building next door. One of the boys waved to me; I waved back.

We walked into the small lobby. It was very dark. We couldn't read the names on the bells.

"Do you have a match, Tony?"

"No."

We walked outside again. The man was leaning on his shovel, watching his young sons work. He smiled as they toiled.

Basillio and I walked over to them. "Can you tell me which apartment Frank Loeb lives in?" I asked.

"Are you police?"

The question took me aback.

"No, of course not."

"Then who?"

"Just friends."

He smiled. "Not good friends?" It was a kind of taunt.

"What the hell is up with this guy? What's he getting at?" Tony muttered in my ear.

"Actually we are good friends of Frank's," I lied.

"Then why would you want to see him? If you were good friends, you would know he was murdered four weeks ago ... wouldn't you? You would know someone threw him down the stairs in his building and ripped his apartment off. You would know he broke his neck."

My anger flared up for just a moment at his response. But then I slipped into Alice Nestleton, actress on demand. I placed my hand gently on his arm and said, "Please help me out. It's very important that I talk to someone who knew Frank Loeb."

His basic Hispanic chivalry toward women came rushing to the surface. "Go back into the lobby," he said. "Press the third bell from the top. That's Mrs. Boyle's apartment. She was a friend of his. She'll tell you all you want to know. In fact, you won't be able to shut her up."

Mrs. Boyle's third-floor apartment was cramped with bulky mahogany pieces that cast gloomy shadows. She picked up a few magazines from two armchairs in the dark living room and invited us to sit. Her chubby black cat, whom she called Augusta, fixed penetrating green eyes on Basillio. Mrs. Boyle—a bustling heavyset woman who wore a wool hat against the chill in the apartment—was a sort of generic old lady, perhaps seventy-five, perhaps ninety.

She served us the worst cup of instant coffee I had ever tasted. She seemed delighted to have the company. I didn't exactly lie to her. When she asked why we were inquiring about the late Frank Loeb, I said that Tony and I had been hired by friends of Mr. Loeb's to find out what had happened.

Mrs. Boyle told us all about the murder and what the police were saying about it: About a month ago Frank Loeb had intervened when neighborhood gang kids were beating a homeless man. The gang members had vowed vengeance. They had broken into the building, trashed his apartment, and flung him down the stairs. The police thought they probably meant only to rough him up, scare him. But the fall killed him. No arrests had been made yet.

I knew it might be painful, I told the elderly woman, but I would find it enlightening if she told me everything she knew about Frank Loeb. Obviously I had touched on one of Mrs. Boyle's favorite topics, because once she began to talk about Loeb, there seemed to be no stopping her. She went on for ninety minutes without a breather, preparing more instant coffee while she talked. Midway through her monologue I noticed that both Tony and Augusta had fallen fast asleep.

But I learned a great deal. I learned that Frank Loeb was beyond a doubt Sustenance House's guardian angel.

As for the man himself—well, he had come to New York, to Mrs. Boyle's building, twenty-five years ago, a dropout from Princeton who wanted to play the flute professionally. He gave up that dream within a few years, though. He was reclusive and seemed to be a man of little means. In fact he lived like a pauper. He had revealed to Mrs. Boyle that he received $150,000 a year from a family trust fund but gave virtually all of it away.

Mrs. Boyle didn't believe him, but it seemed a harmless enough lie, she thought. His only pleasures seemed to be movies, city bus rides, and his cats. He had two Siamese cats that for some reason he had named Tiny and Tim. Odder still was the fact that he had given male names to the obviously female cats, who were sisters. Sadly the cats had vanished on the day he was murdered. His only living relative was a sister in Chicago, from whom he had long been estranged. Mrs. Boyle had thought of him almost like a son and missed him terribly.

"So this whole thing was a waste of time," Tony said as he and I walked down the stairs leading to the sidewalk. "The money orders weren't lost in the mail. There was no change of heart. The poor bastard just got himself killed before he could send this year's donation."

I didn't speak a word as we walked along the busy street. We took the Second Avenue bus downtown. We stopped in at an Irish pub at Second and Fifty-fourth Street. I made the call to Jack Rugow and told him the bad news. He was unhappy to hear what had happened, of course, but still he thanked me profusely for my efforts and told me if I ever needed a favor . . .

I was about to tell him I didn't need a favor, I needed a part, but I decided against such naked aggression.

Then I rejoined Tony at the bar. He finally got his hamburger and was unhappy with it. I just had a long ginger ale with a piece of lime and watched the intermittent snow through the window. The jukebox was playing "Jingle Bell Rock."

"That's that!" Tony said, pushing his plate away. On the face of it, he meant he had given up on the hamburger, but what he was really talking about was Frank Loeb, the anonymous acronym.

Tony was dead wrong.

Chapter 3

Two days later I found a strange little packet in my mailbox. It looked like one of those mailers the banks use to send you a new supply of deposit slips or checks. But I still had plenty of both.

I opened the package standing over the dining room table, my cats looking on. They always seem interested in my mail, as a matter of fact. Perhaps all that tearing of envelopes reminds them of some fantasy home with nothing but cardboard sardine cans, easily clawed open.

I emptied the contents of the package onto the table. And I jumped back in horror.

There was a candy cane inside, wrapped in cellophane. Just like the ones that Will Holland had tried to distribute in a bizarre ritual, before he killed himself.

Now it lay on *my* table.

Embarrassed by my fear, I quickly picked it up and noticed there was a piece of paper attached to the candy with a rubber band.

I peeled off the little typed note: "SUNDAY. 2 P.M. THE BARKING ARK."

What a peculiar note, I thought. What a peculiar package, for that matter.

Now, I knew what the Barking Ark was: a charming pet supply store on Second Avenue that sold all kinds of cat and dog food and equipment. But it was famous for running an adoption agency for stray cats and dogs. Every Sunday these beasties were exhibited to be adopted.

Someone obviously wanted to meet me on Sunday at two. But why the mystery? Why not just pick up the phone and call me, request a meeting?

The more I stared at the candy cane, the more mysterious the note became. Because I really couldn't tell if it was the exact kind of candy cane that Will Holland had thrown on the table. If it was, then maybe someone who had attended that board of directors' meeting was trying to tell me something, to get my attention—or frighten me.

And when all was said and done, why meet at a pet shop?

There was no return address on the packet, the postmark was obscured, and there was absolutely nothing else in the envelope.

It was three days until Sunday, and believe me, during every hour of those three days I thought about this mysterious request for a two p.m. meet at the Barking Ark. It began to obsess me so that I couldn't even eat the candy cane and I had long conversations with Bushy and Pancho late at night about marketing, perhaps a candy cane for cats.

No matter how much I turned it around in my head I could not guess who was going to be waiting for me at the shop. Or why this person wanted to see me.

Sunday arrived. I dressed in a snowsuit, although it had stopped snowing. I entered the Barking Ark fifteen minutes before the appointed time.

The store itself is bifurcated. One side contains the cans of food, the carriers, toys, trinkets, bags of dry dog and cat food with exotic names, vitamin supplements, and so on.

The other side is the adoption setup: large, spotlessly clean cages containing for the most part felines of all sizes, shapes, pedigrees, and ages. Only a few canines.

The "orphanage" was crowded. The retail side was sparse. I waited in the latter area, making believe I was seriously interested in the ingredients in the newer cat food health products.

I was oddly excited, as if I were on a blind date.

The time passed very slowly. The small print on the labels began to blur. At two o'clock I moved to the catnip toys.

At two-fifteen, to the expensive leather carriers with rhinestone studs.

At two-thirty I realized I had been stood up, but I still hadn't the slightest idea who my date was to have been.

At two forty-five I decided it was time to leave.

As I was heading for the door, I had the strangest feeling that I was being watched. I stopped in my tracks and began to turn slowly. No . . . I saw no one.

Starting toward the door again, I felt a gaze again. This time I looked over into the adoption section.

Yes. Two pairs of eyes were fixed on me. They belonged to two lovely Siamese cats that were staring at me from one of the cages.

I walked over to them. "Are you by any chance Tiny and Tim?" I asked.

They were lying side by side.

I didn't know why the names of Frank Loeb's cats came to mind. And I didn't know why I was starting to feel nervous and, frankly, a little afraid.

I walked over to one of the clerks, a short, slim woman wearing what looked like a butcher's apron. "Do you know the names of those Siamese?" I asked.

"Names?" She laughed. "They just came in. We haven't named them yet. I'm hoping someone adopts them before we have to think up names."

"May I ask where they came from?"

She shrugged. "They were left in front of the store. Just like that. No note. No nothing. That isn't usually the way our animals come to us, like out-of-wedlock babies. But look at them. They're beautiful, aren't they? Purebreds too. They've obviously been very well cared for. Are you interested in giving them a home?"

Before I could answer, one of her coworkers called to her. She excused herself, signaling with her hand that she would be back shortly.

I stared at the two Siamese. They calmly returned my look.

All kinds of messages were surfacing. Some rational. Some wild. Some frightening.

The person who had sent me the candy cane wanted me to know the cats were here. That person had never intended to meet with me.

It stood to reason that the same person had left the cats in front of the Barking Ark. It made all the sense in the world.

The thing was, Had that person also killed Frank Loeb?

Most troubling of all, I had the strong feeling that the candy cane itself was a message to me, that the suicide of Will Holland had something to do with the murder of Frank Loeb.

My head reeled. I felt dizzy. I walked out of the store. A bracing cold wind put a spring in my step.

One thing had to be done quickly, I felt.

I walked to the pay phone on the corner, slipped in a quarter, and dialed Tony Basillio's number. He lived only two blocks away from the Barking Ark—in my old apartment.

Tony picked up the phone on the third ring.

His voice was groggy. "You woke me," he said, his voice slurred.

"What are you doing in bed at three in the afternoon, Basillio?"

"The two young actresses I brought home last night just won't let me up."

"Very funny."

"Actually I was having a long, beautiful dream. Stravinsky was in my apartment offering me a million and a half to step out of the theater and into ballet. He wanted me to design a wild new set for *Firebird*."

"Stravinsky's dead, Tony."

"So I understand, Miss Nestleton. But it was a dream."

"Listen, I'm two blocks away."

"Get up here."

"No. You come down."

"What for?"

"I want you to become a foster parent."

He laughed heartily, until he realized that I was only half joking. "Maybe you'd better explain that remark," he said.

"I want you to adopt two cats. They're at the pet store, the Barking Ark."

There was a long, pained silence. Poor Tony.

"Please say you're kidding," he said finally.

This time I fell silent.

"You're not kidding, are you?"

"No, Tony. I'm not."

"Why would I want to adopt two cats? What am I supposed to do with two cats?"

"Feed them, talk to them, love them, learn from them. For starters."

"I don't know what you're up to, madam. But the answer is no. A firm, unqualified, unequivocal, violent no. I don't even get along with your two cats. Everybody knows the sane one hates me and the crazy one thinks I'm the night nurse on his ward."

I put another quarter into the slot and began to list the favors he owed me and the kinds of activities I could engage in against his character and body if he refused.

"Aw, jeez, Alice. Please don't make me adopt two cats. Please?"

Ten minutes later he joined me in the Barking Ark. No more than twenty minutes after that, the four of us were trudging up the stairs to his apartment, me toting the kits and Tony loaded down with bags of kitty litter and food.

Once inside, I immediately opened the carriers.

Tiny and Tim stepped out, looked around, found a quiet corner, and began grooming each other.

"How do you know for sure they're the Loeb cats?"

"I don't," I told Tony.

"Look at them!" He was almost shouting. "Just look at them. Why don't they look confused, or scared, or something? Why are they so damn cool?"

"Give them some water," I said.

"What kinds of names are those anyway: Tiny and Tim? I mean, we're looking at two lady cats here, right? I'm not going to call a girl Tim."

"Actually, my grandmother had a cousin named Timothea. Everyone called her Tim."

"But that was Minnesota."

I decided to overlook that remark. "And Tiny could simply be a corruption of Tina."

"Or," Tony suggested, "poor dead Frank Loeb may really have thought he was living in *A Christmas Carol*. Everything else he did seemed to be unreal."

"Shame on you, Tony. Are you suggesting that Scrooge and Tiny Tim are not real?"

Tony went to get water for his new friends. They watched him curiously. My! What self-sufficient creatures they were. I wondered when they were going to inspect their new home.

I picked up the phone, dialed information, and got the number for the Rep, Jack Rugow's theatrical group. I needed to speak to him.

Jack seemed happy to hear from me. I asked him how Devries had taken the news of Loeb's death.

He was sad, Jack told me, like everyone else, but determined to find other sources of funding. And everyone was marveling at how I had been able to track him down with so little information to go on. Finally there was talk about putting up memorial plaques in the Sustenance House facility for both Will Holland and Frank Loeb.

He took a long breath, then said, "You know, I guess we'll never really know absolutely one hundred percent that Loeb was the one who sent in the money. But I believe he did, and I keep thinking about what a strange man he must have been. I keep trying to think what went on in his mind."

"That kind of anonymity, that desire for privacy, is always strange," I said.

"You know, Alice, there was some talk around about creating a defense fund."

"For whom?"

"For Loeb's murderer, if and when he is caught and charged."

"But why, Jack?"

"Oh, you know. A kind of . . . Christian gesture. In keeping with the season. Love your enemy. Do not seek vengeance. Peace on earth. All that."

"I suppose it does make sense," I replied. Then I got to the point. "Jack, I want to talk to the board again."

"About what?"

"Well, it's not really important. It's just a project I want to do."

"A project?"

It was an easy-to-swallow cock-and-bull story I outlined for him. "Yes, Jack, a play. I was fascinated by that conversation you and Raya what's her name had after the Will Holland tragedy. The conversation about ritual, about Holland's presenting the candy canes and the water pistols as gifts before killing himself. I want to write a play about a man on the verge of suicide . . . and the rituals he is confronted with . . . in life and in his mind. The daily rituals . . . and finally the deadly rituals. I know I'm not making sense. I haven't thought it out really. But do you understand where I'm going?"

"It's a brilliant idea."

"So I just want to interview each of them about what they thought then—and now—about those candy canes slithering across the table toward them."

"I'm sure we'd all be happy to cooperate. The trouble is, Alice, there will be no more meetings until after the new year. But if you want to grab each one individually, you can, any evening, at Sustenance House, between four-thirty and seven."

"But I thought you said there would be no meetings."

"That's right. But there's a tradition at Sustenance House that during the last two weeks before Christmas the members of the board get down in the trenches with the real people. We all become volunteers in the feeding program. And we start at four-thirty." He laughed. "Can you ladle soup?"

"With the best of them," I said.

"Okay. See you tomorrow. Four-thirty. Walk right in."

I hung up. Tony was seated in his chair staring

at me in puzzlement. "What was that all about?" he asked.

"You were listening. You heard."

"Are you serious about writing a play?"

"Of course not. I just needed an excuse."

"Why didn't you tell the truth?"

"Jack might not have been too happy with the truth. I believe now that there was a connection between the suicide of Holland and the murder of Loeb. It was one of those people who sent me the candy cane and sent me to Barking Ark, so I—"

"Hold it a minute!" Tony interrupted. "What candy cane?"

All I had told him was that the cats from the Barking Ark were Loeb's. Now I filled him in on everything that had transpired in the world and in my head since that packet came in the mail for me.

"A candy cane does not a causal chain make," he noted.

"How philosophical of you, Tony. I never knew you had it in you."

He was about to respond when suddenly there was some activity with his new roommates.

Tiny, at least I think it was Tiny, began to rub

her back along his leg, purring beautifully, as if she had found the most heavenly leg of all.

And Tim leaped lightly onto Tony's lap and curled up.

Tony stared at me wide-eyed. He didn't know what to say. Neither did I.

Chapter 4

I did indeed start on the soup line. Jack stood next to me. "We monitor all new volunteers as a matter of course, Alice." He laughed. "But to be honest, you might *need* monitoring. I never met an actress who could really ladle soup."

"You're looking at one," I replied huffily.

The soup was cabbage soup, and it smelled delicious. The ladle was well turned. The soup pot rested on boxes. I sat on a stool. The homeless came past me with paper bowls on plastic trays. I filled the bowl three quarters of the way up.

Jack kept smiling and nodding as if I were his successful protégée.

As for the people whose bowls I filled with cabbage soup, they confused me. Some looked absolutely destitute and derelict. Others simply looked poor. A few looked quite mad.

Down the line I could see the other volunteers manning their stations: bread, meat loaf and gravy, vegetables, pies, coffee. The volunteers looked as raffish as the guests. Even the members of the board of directors—I could see them all from my soup station—seemed to have donned a variety of kooky hats. Wasn't Raya Lambert a hat designer? But it was doubtful if these were her designs. Ishmael Rood wore a Captain Ahab hat. Samuel Mortimer wore a stovepipe. The others were like no hats I had ever seen before— indescribable. I guess it was another one of those strange Sustenance House traditions that Jack kept telling me about.

During serving, the entire first floor of Sustenance House was turned into a cafeteria. Once the two small lunchroom-type rooms were filled, the people ate their food standing up, sitting along the walls, anywhere.

When the maximum density was reached, the line at the door was held up until others left.

"Are you enjoying yourself?" Jack asked.

"More or less," I replied.

"The regular volunteers, the people from the

neighborhood, love the soup station. Me, I love every stop on the line. Isn't it an amazing meal, Alice? There's nothing in New York like Sustenance House. Sure, you can get bologna sandwiches at a lot of soup kitchens. And even good soup. But no other place serves such meals to the homeless, day in, day out. Full-course, hot, nutritious meals. And if you saw our Christmas dinner, Alice, you wouldn't believe it."

His eyes almost misted over. "Seven hundred goose dinners, Alice. It's an extravaganza of love. It should win a Tony and an Emmy and an Oscar."

Suddenly turmoil erupted near the front door. I caught a glimpse of that woman with the disheveled hair, Daisy Eidan, in the middle of things. Then I saw David Devries and a security guard in a blue shirt with a makeshift badge rush into the fray. It was over as quickly as it started.

Jack Rugow explained. "It was probably a homeless person who refused to leave his belongings in the front room while eating. That's one of Daisy's jobs: to help Security keep duffel bags outside."

Devries waved and smiled to me as he walked back to his bread station on the line.

I started my quest. "Jack, could I ask you a few questions about my project?"

"Oh, you mean that idea for the play. Sure. I love it. A kind of ritual drama à la Genet."

I realized that I had to cover the cover story, so I came up with a little nonsense at first.

"Was there anything that you knew about Will Holland that could have led one to predict he would have chosen candy canes and water pistols for his suicide ritual?"

After I asked the question, I realized it wasn't nonsense at all.

Jack pondered the question seriously, then said, "I suppose, in retrospect, it was his commentary on the state of the world. After all, he was a travel writer and he had to entice tourists to foreign countries by stretching the truth a bit. For example, 'Go to Nicaragua. You'll find a little starvation but also delicious rock candy. El Salvador? You'll find death squads but also lovely children playing with water pistols.' Does that make any sense to you, Alice?"

No, it didn't. But I didn't tell him. Now I threw away the cover story and went after hard facts.

"Was that what he wrote, Jack? Travel guides?"

"He wrote articles too, I think. For those fancy travel magazines. But he made his money from the travel guides. One of them was called, I believe, *London on the Cheap*. Budget guides. And a lot of South American ones. He coauthored them with a guy named Justin Walters."

I ladled the soup faster. Now we were getting somewhere.

"Tell me, Jack. Did he ever talk to you about the anonymous donor?"

"We all talked about him, Alice."

"I mean in a special kind of way."

"Like what?"

"As if he knew who Frank Loeb was."

"No."

A homeless woman barked at me for skimping on her portion of soup. I apologized.

"What are you getting at?" Jack asked suspiciously.

"Oh, nothing. Just curious." I smiled at him. "Did you eat your candy cane?"

"What? You mean, the one Will slid across the table that day?"

"That's right."

"No, I didn't eat it. I don't know what happened to it."

"Did Will Holland ever mention Siamese cats to you?"

He looked at me as if I were insane. "What a

weird question. Kind of comes out of left field, doesn't it? Siamese cats? I don't think so. But what the hell do Siamese cats have to do with anything?"

"Frank Loeb had two Siamese. They vanished on the day of his death."

Jack shrugged. "So what?"

"Again, Jack, just asking. Did Will Holland ever mention—"

"No," he said abruptly. "He never discussed Siamese cats with me. Or polecats or hepcats or any other kind of cats."

Jack was getting irritated, and it showed. It was time to move on down the line. I handed him the ladle. He accepted it graciously. Then I stepped back and caught my breath.

Peering down the feeding line, I realized what an enormous and virtually impossible task I had set for myself: to interrogate, artfully, the entire board of directors.

And here they were. Devries at the bread station. Mortimer at the meat loaf. Lambert at the veggies. Rood on dessert. And I had just left Rugow on soup.

But I had to do it now. When would I get them all together again?

Quickly, silently, I formulated the three basic questions:

> *One.* Did the suicide ever exhibit an obsessive interest in the donor?
>
> *Two.* Did you eat your candy cane? The one the suicide gave you as a gift before he pulled the trigger?
>
> *Three.* Did Will Holland ever bring up the subject of Siamese cats?

Honest answers would be important. But I was really after any kind of bizarre response. A sudden shift in body language. A sudden chill.

I walked over to David Devries. He was offering biscuits or white bread. He greeted me warmly. I told him how happy I was to help out. Then I casually asked him the three questions. He didn't seem to find it at all odd; he just answered no to all three. I picked up nothing from his manner.

Then on to Samuel Mortimer. He was forking out meat loaf slabs with one hand and gravy with the other. It looked luscious. He was happy for company. He listened bemused to my three questions, gave unqualified noes to all, and then remarked in a conspiratorial fashion, "You know, after the shock of the suicide wears off, one finds oneself fascinated with the man. I understand your curiosity."

So I moved down the line to Raya Lambert and her trio of vegetables: honey-glazed carrots, peas with bacon, and sweet potato puree. No wonder there were long lines outside Sustenance House. The place fed well.

She was a problem, Raya. She did not like my questions. Her handsome, chiseled face turned stony when she heard the first one. I was rather startled.

"Why are you asking me this nonsense?" she snapped.

Before I could respond, she added: "We gave you the authority to find our anonymous bene-factor, and you accomplished the task. You did a brilliant job. But the man is dead. So be it. Case closed. What gives you the right to continue in-vestigating . . . whatever it is that you're investi-gating. You're obviously up to something. What is it? In addition to that, I find your questions silly and patronizing. Did I eat my candy cane! Are you joking? Who the hell could remember something like that after—after . . . We all had other things on our minds. Don't you remember?"

I stepped away from her. She continued to serve the line of people filing past her. She refused to look at me. Time to move on—again.

The final station was the dessert and coffee stop, manned by Ishmael Rood.

I hesitated. What should I make of Raya Lambert's angry outburst? It was what I was looking for: an unexpected response to the questions. But somehow I felt that her anger did not implicate her. I simply could not imagine her sending me a candy cane.

Then I walked to Rood's station. The dessert was not in the same class as the rest of the menu. It was typical supermarket apple pie, obviously donated to Sustenance House after the freshness date had expired.

"There is only one restaurateur on the board of directors," Rood said wryly. "Why would they ask me to hand out this abomination?" He kept his voice low so that the diners could not hear him.

I changed the subject, complimenting him on the ridiculous hat.

He laughed. "David gave it to me. He's old-fashioned. 'Servers must wear hats,' he said. Do you know where that tradition comes from?"

"No."

"The military. A hygiene precaution. So that lice, dandruff, and other execrables do not fall into the food and start an epidemic . . . or a riot. I wonder if they still do it."

He chuckled and seemed lost in a memory. Rood was a handsome man of about fifty, with olive skin and dark black hair that he wore long. His eyes seemed to glint all the time. He looked much taller than he really was because he carried himself like a maître d'—imperiously.

He gave a very quick no to each of my questions. Then he said, almost apologetically, "To be honest, Will and I rarely spoke. We had maybe two or three conversations in all the time we were acquainted with each other. Mostly about the strange phenomenon that the English simply cannot learn how to cook. Of course, it all had to do with his famous guide *London on the Cheap*. He used to make a joke about fish and chips. But I forget it."

I thanked him and started to walk back to my station.

"Just a minute, Miss Nestleton."

"Yes?"

"I don't know why we never got friendly. It

was odd. I mean, I saw him more often than the other board members did."

"Why was that?"

"He used to eat in my restaurant. On Columbus Avenue. And I'll tell you something else. I saw him several times with women. At no time did he ever look depressed. He seemed to be enjoying himself immensely with his dates. Chronic depression? Who knows? But I never saw it."

"You mean, in your restaurant? You mean, he always came in to eat with women?"

"Yes. There were two of them. He seemed to alternate."

"Who were they? Do you know?"

"I don't. They both looked a bit older than he was. But even I like older women. No insult intended, but they're warmer. Like main dishes rather than appetizers."

I gritted my teeth and said nothing concerning his views on womankind.

"Did you know their names?"

"He introduced me. All I remember is that one was named Annette."

"Annette," I repeated softly. A homeless man, unhappy with his slice, told Ishmael Rood that he would very much like the corner piece. He looked apologetic to be making such a request. But Ishmael replaced the center cut with the corner happily. The man trudged on.

Rood turned to me, grinning. "I like people who judge food critically. No matter what their temporary station in life."

"Were you ever down and out?" I asked.

"Does a mousse need eggs?" he retorted.

I thanked him and headed back to relieve Jack at the soup station. I was elated. Finally there was something to think about, explore, puzzle out. Annette. Rood was right. Really depressed people simply do not eat out often. Too much energy is required. And if they do, it's usually alone. Oh, this was definitely a contradiction that had to be resolved. It wasn't the kind of information I was seeking. It didn't explain anything—much like the candy cane or the cats—but it was a wedge.

And I knew exactly where to go next. Will Holland's collaborator, Justin Walters, the man Jack had mentioned. And the man David Devries had probably talked about, the man who had provided the police with information about Will Holland's state of mind.

I left immediately after finishing the serving and treated myself to a cab ride home through the festooned pre-Christmas streets. New York is truly a wondrous sight as a holiday approaches.

Weary but happy with the fact that my inquiry had yielded fruit no matter how sparse, I trudged up the stairs. Tomorrow I would look up Mr. Justin Walters, coauthor of—what was it called?—yes, the perennial best-seller *London on the Cheap*.

The moment I opened the door I saw Bushy waiting for me, eyes glowering. He was hungry. Pancho was too busy to bother.

"Yes, yes," I said. "I'm back."

Just as I was stepping through the door, I sensed a strange light over my right shoulder.

I turned and stepped back into the hallway, horrified.

Someone had graffitied the entire concrete wall running parallel to my apartment!

I stepped back outside. The graffiti was extensive, not done in the usual subway fashion with spray paint. This was done with brilliantly colored chalk.

There were two human figures: a beautiful golden-haired woman in medieval garb and a handsome dark prince, sword at his side, kneeling and kissing her hand.

Next to the woman were two cats: a big Maine coon and a gray cat with half a tail.

On the top of the wall was a printed border. It read:

SIR TONY CONFESSES HIS LOVE FOR THE BEAUTEOUS LADY NESTLETON.

My God! I thought. Had Basillio flipped his lid?

I closed the door softly behind me and fed the cats. Twice that evening, before I went to bed, I stepped out into the hall to study Tony's love letter. I just didn't know how to deal with it.

Well, I thought, I'll wash it off when we have our next fight . . . or after Christmas, whichever is sooner.

Chapter 5

It was not easy to find Justin Walters. The NYPD detectives who had spoken to him wouldn't give out any information at all. Even when I used David Devries's name as a reference. He wasn't in the Manhattan phone book. The receptionist at his publisher's was noncooperative; she suggested I write to him care of the company.

Only a bit of chicanery helped. I simply called the publicity department of his publisher and identified myself as a professor at the City University writing a long article on travel writing in American literature for the *New York Times Magazine*. I got an address and telephone number immediately.

Justin Walters worked in a small office, right around the corner from the main branch of the public library at Forty-second Street. There were two work spaces in the place; one of them had obviously been Will Holland's.

The walls were covered with blown-up covers of old Holland and Walters guidebooks. There were three high bookshelves filled with maps, books, and audiocassettes. There was a fax machine and two small copiers. In the center of all this clutter was a high stool on which sat an electric percolator.

Justin Walters was a chubby man with one of those bowl haircuts. He had to be older than he looked.

"How did you find me?" he asked suspiciously, closing his laptop.

"Your publicity people," I replied.

He eyed me up and down. For some reason there was a sudden mutual dislike between us. It was just one of those things.

"And you want to see me concerning what?" he asked. He wore a beautiful pair of granny glasses.

I didn't know what to say, so I asked a nonsense question to break the ice. "Did you and Will ever do a guidebook to Finland?"

It didn't work. He narrowed his eyes, kept silent, and began to tap the top of the machine.

So then I got to the point. "I know Will Holland had two close women friends. I need their names and addresses."

"Oh, do you?" He all but curled his lip.

"Yes, it's important."

"Important for whom, and why?"

Oh! This was going to be like pulling teeth. "Well, Mr. Walters, I could give you any number of reasons why I need the information. All of them good."

"Name one."

"I think you told the police something less than the truth concerning Will Holland's state of mind before he killed himself."

The man actually smiled. "Get out of here or I'll call Building Security," he said.

"Maybe I can give you a better reason."

"You'd better."

"Let's just say that before he took his own life, Will Holland learned he was about to be involved in a very messy paternity suit. And I mean messy. Moreover, this mess might drag a lot of other people down along with him. So all I can say is that the more his friends cooperate, the less I'll harass them."

It was a totally outrageous fabrication. But I

was desperate. And it worked. Not immediately, of course.

He stared at me. He seemed to be evaluating the truth of my assertion. He stared and glared and took some coffee and tied a shoelace.

Then he said, "I don't believe you."

I was silent.

Then he said, "But it's no skin off my back."

Then he pointed.

"Do you see that small desk?"

"Yes."

"Will worked there. In the top right drawer is a sheet of white legal-size paper. It's his Christmas gift list. There are seven names and addresses on it. Only three in New York City: me and two women."

I walked to the desk, extracted the paper, made a copy of it, and replaced the original.

Then I looked at the names.

Isabel Mizrachi. She lived on West 103d Street.

Annette Vlakos. Twelfth Street and Second Avenue.

"He gave the same Christmas present every year to everyone on his list. A fifty-dollar bottle of cabernet sauvignon."

"Did he ever talk to you about a Frank Loeb?" I asked, pressing my luck.

"What's that? A wine?"

I walked out. The piece of paper was generating heat in my palm.

Seated on the ledge of my window, I watched the darkness fall. Bushy was next to me. Pancho was flying about the loft in one of his lunatic runs from unseen enemies.

The reproduced sheet of paper with the names and addresses of Holland's Christmas gift obligations lay between Bushy and me. I had already memorized the relevant names: Annette Vlakos and Isabel Mizrachi. They would know my name tomorrow.

I waited until it was dark and then called Tony.

"How are your new friends?" I asked.

"You mean Natasha and Heloise?"

"No. I mean Tiny and Tim."

He laughed. "Everyone is getting along fine."

"Are they eating?"

"Yes. They like the turkey and giblet cans best. But after all, they don't eat much. They're very proper ladies, you know."

"Speaking about being proper, Tony . . . look . . .

I appreciate the sentiment, but please don't make any more large-scale pastel drawings in my building."

"Did you like it?" he asked eagerly.

"Of course. But that's not the point. I think—"

He was off and running. "At first I thought of making your hair burnt sienna—a kind of metaphor for beauty—but then I thought—"

"Whoa, Tony, whoa!"

"What?"

"Have you been drinking excessively, Tony?"

"No. Not at all. Why do you ask?"

For some reason I just couldn't flat out say to him that he was acting strange. After all, he had made a beautiful mural. But something was going on with him. Maybe his ex-wife was pressuring him too hard. Maybe . . . maybe . . . well, he was in the theater.

"Come over, Alice," he urged. "Stay with me tonight. We all miss you."

I laughed. "Who is 'we'?"

"The cats and me."

"Tony, those cats don't even know me. And they've only been living with you for two days."

"They talk about you constantly, Swede. I hear

their conversations. About how you rescued them from danger."

"Tony, they were not in any danger. The Barking Ark was a safe haven."

There was a long silence. He seemed to have broken the connection.

"Tony! Tony, are you there?"

"Yes, I'm here. Listen, Alice, just come on over. Spend the night with me. I long for you."

"What an old-fashioned way of putting it, Tony. Delightful to the ear."

"Then you'll come?"

"No."

"Why not?"

"I have to be up and out early tomorrow morning."

"Why?"

"A break in the case."

"What case?"

"Sustenance House, of course."

"Swede," he said with a sigh, "the poor will always be with us. But love withers with the body's decay."

"Tony, do you know how strange you are beginning to sound?"

"Strange? I have always depended on the quality of strangeness, Miss Nestleton."

"Okay," I said reluctantly, not understanding at all. "I have to go now, Tony. I'll call you tomorrow."

"Wait!"

"Yes?"

"Have you fed your cats?"

"Of course I have. In fact I fed them hours earlier than usual. Bushy was driving me mad."

"One more question. What should I get them for Christmas?"

"Get who? The cats, you mean?"

"Right."

"Let your pocket be your guide, Tony. Bushy is fond of hand-carved brushes and combs, and Pancho can never get his fill of beat poetry. Give him a Kerouac book and a cup of strong coffee, and he's in heaven."

Tony didn't laugh.

"I feel wonderful, Swede," he said. "Really good."

"That's excellent, Tony."

"I feel at peace with the world—you know?"

"That's what it's all about, Tony. I mean, this season. That's the way you're supposed to feel at this time."

Actually, I didn't believe he was listening to me at all.

"And you, Swede, how do you feel?"

"Confused, Tony. Good night for now."

At nine-thirty the next morning I boarded the uptown bus on Hudson Street. I left the bus at 96th and Central Park West. It was a short walk to 103d at Amsterdam, where Isabel Mizrachi lived.

The apartment house was huge and old. The doorman was young, with a starched but faded green uniform. He sat behind a high desk in the lobby. "May I help you?" he asked.

"I'm here to see Isabel Mizrachi."

"Is she expecting you?" He had a slight foreign accent that was utterly charming.

My reply was an honest one. "I don't really know."

"Your name?"

I gave him my name, and he picked up the house phone and rang her.

There was a brief conversation that I couldn't hear. Then he turned his attention to me again. "She wants to know what this is pertaining to."

"It's personal."

He spoke into the receiver again, then listened

more, and finally hung up. "She'll be down," he announced. He pointed across the lobby to a sofa. I walked over there and took a seat.

A few minutes later a stout fiftyish woman wearing a yellow sweater walked out of the elevator. Her short graying hair was beautifully styled. She looked at the doorman, and he gestured toward me.

As Isabel Mizrachi approached, I started to rise. She signaled with an abruptly raised hand that I should remain seated. "What did you say your name was?" she asked me.

"Alice Nestleton."

"I'm sorry, I don't know who you are."

"Well, we've actually never met. But we have a mutual friend."

"Who?"

"Will Holland."

She did not reply. She began to look me over in a critical fashion, as if evaluating me. But I couldn't pick up the criteria.

"Then you know he's dead," she finally said.

"Yes. I was there when it happened. At Sustenance House. I would like to talk to you about him. I want—"

She halted me with another firm traffic cop–type

gesture. "It was interesting meeting you, Miss Nestleton," she said. With that she turned on her heel and headed back to the elevator bank.

What was that all about? What was the matter with the woman? I jumped up and, furious at her bad manners, started to pursue her.

But the doorman moved out threateningly from behind his counter. I stopped short. Isabel was pressing the up button.

"Frank Loeb!" I called out on impulse. "Did you know Frank Loeb?"

She was inside the car now, facing me, but refused to look directly at me.

The elevator doors were beginning to close like a final curtain.

"Tiny Tim!" I shouted.

Isabel was gone. I glared at the doorman, who merely shrugged. I walked out of the building and headed for the subway nearby.

Annette Vlakos lived on Twelfth Street between Second and First avenues. The building was trim and well kept. Her basement apartment was separated from the street by a small set of steps and an iron grate, and her door was in a tiny courtyard containing an old cement planter that now functioned as an umbrella stand.

I spotted the bell atop the newly painted iron gate. I rang seven times—long, insistent rings—before Miss Vlakos appeared in the little courtyard.

She was a tall, stoop-shouldered woman, about my age, with long black hair done in twin braids . . . like Pocahontas. She was wearing several sweaters.

"Who are you ringing for?" she asked through the grate.

"Annette Vlakos," I replied.

"I am she."

"My name is Alice Nestleton. I watched Will Holland die. I must talk to you."

For some reason I had whispered the words, and there was urgency and passion in my voice, though I had made no conscious effort at dramatics.

My hands were entwined in the iron grate. She responded to my urgency with a reach of her hand against the grate. Her hand touched mine, but then she pulled it away sharply, as if she rued the brief, compassionate contact.

"What a foolish woman you are to inquire after the dead," she remarked in a kind of horrified voice, as if I were desecrating a tomb.

"There are ramifications," I retorted, and I instantly realized it was the wrong thing to say.

"Ramifications?" she repeated, mocking the almost academic sound of the word. Then she threw her head back and laughed a wild laugh.

"I'm sure there are ramifications beyond our imaginings," she crooned.

Was this woman mad?

Then she began to speak in a low voice that I had to strain to hear. "Would you like a cup of cocoa? I can bring it out for you. And after you finish, just leave the cup on the ground."

"No, thank you. I don't think so."

"Too bad," she whispered again, "because that's all you'll get from me."

Then she was gone, back behind the doors.

I climbed up the steps and stood on the street, glowering at the world. I was obviously in the middle of a losing streak. It was cold and damp, but the weather was inconsequential compared to my disappointment and confusion. I simply didn't know what to do next.

But then it dawned on me to go to Loeb's neighbor, Mrs. Boyle. Maybe she could identify the two women and tell me something about them.

Why hadn't I visited Vlakos first and Mizrachi second? That way I could have just crossed the park uptown to talk to Mrs. Boyle. Obviously I was doing everything wrong. And I didn't feel like going all the way uptown again.

I went in search of a friendly little café a friend had once taken me to in the neighborhood. After a few minutes of wandering and peering in doors, I found the Café Gigi. I ordered a cappuccino, and while it was being made, I used the pay phone.

The moment Mrs. Boyle picked up the phone, she said she didn't have time to talk; she was "on the way to Pioneer." I knew what she meant: the local supermarket.

"I'll take only a moment of your time," I said. I had the feeling that Mrs. Boyle did not remember who I was.

Quickly, rather brilliantly, I thought, I described my two mystery women.

Mrs. Boyle began to breathe heavily as she silently digested my information. Obviously the poor woman was all bundled up for her marketing expedition and already a bit weary.

Finally she said: "No, dearie, I never saw those women here. Frank never had women in his room."

She had to go, she said. Suddenly I realized that I should ask her about Tiny and Tim.

"Just a minute, Mrs. Boyle. Please! There's one more thing. I think I found Frank Loeb's Siamese cats."

"That's the most wonderful news!" She coughed into the receiver. "I will tell Augusta."

Augusta, I recalled, was her cat.

"Did she play with the other two cats?"

"Augusta is not friendly to other cats. But Tiny and Tim tried their best."

"Yes . . . well . . . Mrs. Boyle, listen. I'm not absolutely sure I found Tiny and Tim. Did they have any distinguishing marks?"

"Of course they did. They were lovely little ladies."

"No, I mean physical marks, like clipped ears or a shortened tail."

"Not that I remember. Oh, Eunice, I have to go now."

"Alice, Mrs. Boyle. My name is Alice, not Eunice."

She coughed again, then said in a whisper, "I will tell you a secret. A stranger has been hanging around here. Everyone is frightened. He comes at night, you know, so I can't see his face. He watches the house. Oh, it is scarifying."

"Probably a detective, Mrs. Boyle."

"No, he's not a detective, dearie. He wears a muffler!"

Then the phone clicked off. I returned to my seat and picked up my cup. In spite of the soft dark charm of Café Gigi—there was even a young couple nuzzling and an old poet with a laptop at the corner table—I was growing morose.

To make matters worse, they were playing Lena Horne songs on the sound system, and Lena had moved seamlessly into one of the saddest and most menacing of songs, something about an ill wind blowing.

This had been the first holiday season in a long time that I had been positively happy. Now events and the music were starting to sour it all.

I left the café abruptly, took the Ninth Street bus across town, and got home just a little after one p.m. I had been out only four hours, but I felt as if I had spent twenty-four hours straight in my grandmother's milking shed.

I stared for a moment, unhappily, at Tony's wall art before I opened the door.

Bushy was not there to greet me. Instead Pancho was lolling on his back, grinning at me. Very unusual.

"What are you doing, Panch?" I inquired, shutting the door behind me.

Suddenly I tensed. Something was wrong in my apartment . . . very wrong.

Someone, or something, was in the loft with me and the cats.

My hands began to tremble. I listened. But there was no sound. I turned. My eyes caught flashes of red near the windows.

My hand went involuntarily to my throat. I couldn't believe my eyes. There are eight large windows in my loft. Under each one is a ledge wide enough to sit on comfortably and look out. But sitting there was now impossible because on each of the eight window ledges sat a magnificent oversize poinsettia in full bloom. Someone had broken into my loft and filled it with those fiery red Christmas flowers.

I was too astonished to move. Bushy was calmly chewing on one plant.

It had to have been Tony who did this, I realized. The poor man was going stark raving mad. First the graffiti on the wall in the hallway. Now this. It was getting very uncomfortable being loved so extravagantly, so suddenly, by a man I had known for so long and who was never extravagant when it came to matters of the heart.

I walked wearily to my dining room table and sat down, still wearing my outer garments, including my gloves.

The candy cane, the one that had been sent to me anonymously along with the note about the Barking Ark, lay on top of the table. I pushed it around on the table like a kitten playing with a spool.

Then I turned and stared at the poinsettias. Tony's current foolishness would have to go on the back burner, I realized. I had to concentrate on the candy cane and the Siamese cats, and Will Holland and Frank Loeb—in their graves, violently, prematurely, inexplicably.

The two women had told me nothing. They had refused even to speak to me. But their silence and animosity only confirmed the hunch I had: that there was a connection among all of them. A kind of murderous triangle: Holland on one corner, Loeb on another, and the women on the third.

Something had happened within the triangle, and it added up to more than Christmas candy and purebred kitties.

* * *

In the comfortable leather booth Nora inspected the salt shaker on the table. It was early evening in that poinsettia day. I had journeyed uptown again, this time to Pal Joey's to get some help.

I recounted my visits to the two women in Will Holland's life. Nora found my tale amusing. "Maybe," she noted, "you've lost your interrogatory charm."

She looked around the restaurant then. "Where's Tony?"

"At the moment he's too crazy to be of help."

"What's he done?"

I told her about the wall art and the riot of flowers left in my place.

"Well, I'll be. 'Tis the season, right?"

"Maybe. But he is taking it a bit too far. Wouldn't you agree?"

"Ah, Alice. 'Love's not Time's fool, though rosy lips and cheeks / Within his bending sickle's compass come.' "

I pulled the salt shaker angrily from Nora's hand. "Why is it, Nora, that retired song and dance ladies can quote Shakespeare but retired actresses have no luck whatsoever quoting Gershwin?"

"One of life's mysteries," she said smugly.

"No doubt. But let's forget about Tony for now. I need your help."

"Here I am."

"Both of the women I visited today used to accompany Will Holland to a restaurant on Columbus Avenue. It's owned by a member of Sustenance House's board of directors, Ishmael Rood. I think the place is called the Briny Deep."

"I know the joint. A fish place with a New Orleans chef."

"Good. I thought maybe, if you have an hour or two this evening when you can get away, you could go up there and hang around the bar for a while . . . flirt with the bartender. Maybe he can tell you something."

"Why don't you go, Alice? You're prettier."

"But you're sexier. Besides, you know the secret language of bartending."

She guffawed. "Oh, is that so?"

"Ishmael Rood would find it strange if I showed up and started flirting with his barman."

"Look, I'll give it a try, Alice. You know I take my work as first assistant to Manhattan's foremost dilettante sleuth quite seriously."

Her words startled me. "This is the first time you've ever insulted me, Nora."

"How did I insult you?"

"By calling me a dilettante."

"But, Alice, love, I meant no insult. Believe me. To me, the word applies to anyone who does something for any reason other than love or money. Hell, I *like* dilettantes. They make the world livable. . . . Santa is a dilettante."

"If you say so, Nora."

Then there was one of the usual commotions in the kitchen—voices screeching at each other in Spanish. Nora rushed off to investigate. I smiled to myself. Half the time Nora calms the waters in the Pal Joey bistro. But the other half of the time it is she who has started all the commotion.

She came back to the booth in about five minutes. "Let me get you something to eat, Alice."

"No, thanks. Tony is spending the night. He's bringing some kind of exotic trash for us to eat. Indonesian frankfurters or some such. And given his current lunatic state, who knows what'll be on the menu tonight?"

"How is he getting along with the Bobbsey twins?"

"You mean Tiny and Tim. Well, it seems to be a

match made in heaven. I believe it's fair to say he adores them and the feeling is mutual."

"Ha! When I see it, I'll believe it," she said, adding, "I'll dive into the Briny Deep tonight, Alice. Late. If I learn anything about Mesdames Mizrachi and Vlakos, or their consort, I'll call you in the morning."

I went back downtown to my loft. The red light on the phone machine was blinking lazily. The message was from Basillio, Lord of the Poinsettias.

"I can't make it tonight," he told me hurriedly. "I have to go to New Haven. A job interview. Can you imagine? Me at Yale! But it really is about time they came to their senses and recognized me. A Yale without a Basillio is a contradiction in terms. I'm giving you as a reference, by the way. Ask Jack Rugow when you see him again if he'll lie for me. See you soon, babe. I've told my roommates—both now called Clytemnestra—that you'll be over to feed them a late supper. I told them how lucky they are to receive a visit from the most beautiful, talented, and intelligent—"

Beep. The message ended there.

Well, I had promised him free cat-sitting services as one of the inducements to adopt the two Siamese.

I fed my cats, stared for a while at the eight brilliantly colored plants decorating my windows like sentries, and then took a nap. What a long day this was shaping up to be.

I left the loft around nine in the evening and splurged on a cab to Tony's place, my old place on Twenty-sixth Street. I climbed briskly up the familiar steps, inserted the key, and stepped inside the apartment, flicking on the light switch.

The place was a mess. Well, that came as no surprise. That was Basillio. He had draped his clothing in the strangest places, like over the TV set and on the curtain rods.

The two T's were seated side by side just in front of the end table in the hallway, where Tony kept the phone.

"Expecting a call, ladies?" I asked.

Quickly I began to tidy up. Then I went into the kitchen and fixed up the litter box and looked at what kinds of provisions were left from our original cat food purchase. Tony had obviously not liked my selection. The cans I'd picked out were intact. Foolish Tony had gone out and purchased two dozen of the most expensive variety of cans. What they charged for those little tins was an outrage.

"Well, missies," I announced, "thanks to your very generous papa, on the menu this evening is smoked duck in savory juices."

They were now at the entrance to the kitchen. They should have been fed hours earlier, but they didn't seem at all anxious about supper. My cats would have been turning cartwheels by now.

I filled the water bowls, replenished their dry food supply, and then split the can of smoked duck in two. I stepped back. "Soup's on," I declared.

Tiny started for her food first. At least I thought it was Tiny, but I really could not tell them apart yet.

The little Siamese stopped halfway to the dish, circled back, rubbed herself along my legs, and finally settled across my shoe. She looked up at me and purred lovingly. It was a touching display of feline love and gratitude from a creature that didn't know me at all.

"You're quite welcome, honey," I said, positively glowing.

Then Tim performed the exact same ritual. As I stood looking down at them, one on each foot, for the first time I could spot the subtle differences between them. Tim had smaller ears, and Tiny had a slightly darker hue.

I went into the living room and sat on the sofa after they had begun to eat their repast. My thoughts were on Sustenance House and its strange progeny of death.

I must have still been tired, because I dozed off, only to be wakened a bit later by a pressure on my arm.

One of the cats was on the sofa next to me, and she—probably Tiny—kept rolling her head on and off my arm, as if she wanted to be fondled and scratched.

She was so adorable I just scooped her up and kissed her sweet nose.

Then she leaped lightly down. It was time to go, I thought. Cat-sitting assignment completed.

But then Tim was suddenly next to me.

"Do you want your nose kissed too? Is that it?"

She left my side immediately and climbed up behind me, to the top of the sofa, right behind my head.

"Are you sure you want to sit there, dearie? I'll lean on you, you know. I just might use you as my little Siamese pillow."

I leaned back playfully. All she did was purr happily.

"My goodness, how kind of you," I purred back while she sniffed gently at my hairline.

Wow! There were pillows . . . and there were pillows. There were friendly cats, and there were friendly cats. I bet this one really would have allowed me to use her soft, lush little belly as a place to rest my head.

But it was time for me to go.

Just then the cat jumped down. Ten seconds later her sister jumped up and took her place behind my head. And thus began a wondrous tag team match. They came and went, came and went, at no time leaving me unattended for more than a minute.

"Lord! You two are the most lovesick catties I've ever known." I immediately realized what a stupid thing that was to have said. They were probably just lonely. They missed Frank Loeb.

The moment I got back to my loft, I promised my cats to introduce them to Tiny and Tim. Bushy began grooming himself. Pancho began running.

I fell into a deep sleep. It had been a long, long

day. I was determined to get a full eight hours that night.

Alas, that was not to be. The chickens had already escaped from the coop.

Chapter 6

The telephone woke me at seven-twenty that next morning, its bell about as melodious as an old-time dentist's drill.

I got out of bed in slow motion, making a rude gesture at the insistent ringing. Bushy began to moan those "feed me" blues, and Pancho was scampering around underfoot. All the while the phone continued its annoying peal.

I soon realized I had turned off the answering machine. The phone was going to go on ringing until I picked it up. Finally I did.

It was Nora on the other end. "Wake up, princess," she said.

"I'm up, I'm up—thanks to you."

"Ready for my report?"

"Yeah."

"I went over to the Briny Deep last night and did my vamp shtick with the bar guy. You know, they used to say my legs were as good as Dietrich's, and I used 'em last night, let me tell you. Had him salivating. He spilled just about everything in that head of his. But I'm afraid the pickings were pretty slim."

The sleep was out of my head now. "I'll take any kind of pickings, Nora."

"Are you sure you're conscious, Alice?"

"Yes, I'm wide awake."

"First I have to tell you how I got him salivating."

"By all means."

"Now, you know . . . you damn well know that I've had problems with bartenders in the past at Pal Joey."

"Yes, I'm aware that you fire them with great rapidity."

That was the wrong thing to say. I guess I wasn't thinking clearly.

She exploded. "The ones I fired deserved to be fired. They were either dipping into the till or calling California in prime time on my office phone or loan-sharking on the side. I even had one guy who was a dancer and when he would go on auditions would just bring in any old friend to stand in for him—without asking me and without making sure that said friend knew how to even make a simple Bloody Mary. Believe me, Alice, I know it's a tough job, but they are a cross to bear, those guys."

"Whatever you say, Nora."

"Anyway, I analyzed the situation before going up there. And I said to myself, 'Now, what does the average bartender find sexy? And what's the tip-off that she's available?' Particularly a bartender in that kind of place, where you have people who do the old-fashioned thing: dress up for dinner. It's a nice seafood restaurant, but it isn't very hip. So I say to myself, 'Nora, honey, you're going to have to look a teeny-weeny bit tawdry. To get him thinking. Are you following me, Alice?"

"Yes. Brilliant strategy, Nora." What else could I say?

"So I put on a boa."

"A boa."

"Yep. Found one in the closet, flung it on, and just sauntered in. The minute I take a peek at the bartender I know the poor fool doesn't have a chance. He's dead in the water. There's no way he would be able to withstand my attack. He was about thirty-five, with a little gray hair. Handsome, trim, and—get this, Alice—he had a deep tan."

She paused, as if she were savoring the memory.

"And what happened, Nora?"

"Well, then I was faced with an unanticipated problem. There I was, standing about ten feet from the bar, and I could feel the bartender's eyes all over me. But I had neglected to plan the order. I mean, what was I drinking? It had to be a bit different. Something a tad challenging, something a tad tawdry, something that would give him a little flutter. Do you know what I'm saying, Alice?"

"Sure, oh, of course." I had no idea what she was saying—or not saying—or trying to say.

"Would it be a martini? No way. Jack Daniel's on the rocks? Nuh-uh. No. I wanted to confuse him, dazzle him, entice him. So I figured on that new kind of drink some of the cool people downtown are having. A small glass of fine port and a bottle of bad domestic beer. I sat down at the bar and gave him my order. He was impressed. When he delivered my drink, I delivered the pièce de résistance. I said, 'What kind of place is this?' You know how I said it—like a country girl in the big city who's looking for action. Bartenders love to show how smart and perceptive they are. This one was no different. He starts pontificating about the kind of people who come in to eat and drink. And he really gets into it and starts speaking real low, like what he's telling me is for my ears only and it's important and intimate. And that's when I knew I had him!"

"So?"

She let out a sigh. "The trouble was, Alice, when it came down to brass tacks, his memory was fuzzy. Maybe he sat under the sunlamp too long."

"*So?*" My patience was wearing thin.

"Okay. One of Will Holland's ladies, the tall one, used to wait for him at the bar. She was a chatterer."

"That would be Annette Vlakos," I said, remembering her impressive height.

"She and the bartender chatted about music, he said."

"Music?"

"Yes. About how they both hate rap music."

"And that's it?"

"Yes, I'm afraid so. The only other thing he

ever found out from their chats—I mean, other than that she didn't like rap—was that she taught music briefly at Juilliard. Years ago. Her instrument was the flute."

I felt as if I had been hit suddenly with a huge snowball.

"Alice, are you there?"

"I'm here."

"Look. I'll speak to you later. I have to get down to the Motor Vehicle Bureau."

She hung up. I lay down again and remained there for a long time staring at the ceiling. It was beginning to flake.

How odd it is, I thought, that a tiny, insignificant fact can send a whole carefully built edifice tumbling wildly down. Not the one I had built—no. The evidentiary edifice built by the cops uptown, who thought that Frank Loeb had been murdered by a street gang, the edifice built by the members of Sustenance House's board of directors, who misled me—purposefully or not—when they assured me that there was no connection between Will Holland and the anonymous donor.

I had been right. Absolutely right. There had been a triangle, and now, with that single small fact Nora had unearthed, I could measure all the angles. Not precisely, of course. But enough to know what had happened.

Three aspects of the problem were now crystal-clear:

First. When Frank Loeb arrived in New York twenty years ago to study the flute, he had made the acquaintance of Annette Vlakos at Juilliard.

Second. Annette Vlakos and Will Holland had conspired in some way to kill Frank Loeb. For money . . . for a piece of the many thousands the eccentric recluse gave away each year.

Third. The suicide was probably Will Holland's remorse—his horror at the full consciousness of what he had done—whether it was only Loeb's money or it also had something to do with a romantic love for Annette.

I couldn't prove a damn thing, but I could confront Annette Vlakos and tell her that I *knew*—and then watch the cookie crumble.

But confront her alone?

No. I didn't have enough evidence. And there

were still perplexing problems. Had Annette sent the candy cane to me? Did she have another murderous ally on the board of directors?

All I really had was her guilt. Of that I was sure.

No. I needed help with this. I needed someone with me . . . someone who constituted authority . . . someone of threat and stature . . . someone to let her know what she was up against and that only a full, honest confession would save her from the firing squad.

Bushy wasn't interested in my problems. He wanted his breakfast. He recruited Pancho to wail along with him, and soon it was like an insane asylum.

So I fed them. Then I dressed and walked to Tony's place and fed the lovely sisters.

It was a long, cold walk. I didn't hang around for their tag team love show. I left after filling the dishes and walked into the first coffee shop I saw.

After the second cup and an almond croissant, I had a rather brilliant idea: Harold Rothwax! Why not?

Sure, I hadn't seen this former NYPD homicide detective in a while. But I knew where to find him. He was now the director of security for a

Korean merchants' association whose offices were listed in the phone book.

I had met him years ago, when I worked briefly as a consultant for a specialized unit of the police department called Retro. I had helped solve a gruesome and perplexing string of murders in which a toy mouse was always left by the victim's side.

Rothwax and I always had a good relationship. A whole lot of joking between us. Sometimes he called me Claire. Sometimes I called him Marmaduke. Don't ask me why. I don't know how that got started. But most of the time he referred to me as Cat Woman—half in respect, half in mockery.

Rothwax looked like a cop, talked like a cop. And he was licensed to carry a weapon in his new job.

Yes, he was the companion I needed.

One hour later I was seated in front of a very surprised Rothwax. It was a rather dingy office in an old building on Broadway between Twenty-ninth and Thirtieth streets, a section chock-full of Korean wholesalers, importers, and restaurants.

"I assume, Cat Woman, you are here to deliver my Christmas present."

"No. I always deliver my gifts when and where they're supposed to be delivered. In a sock hanging on a fireplace on Christmas Eve."

He found that funny. But then again, he had always considered me a country bumpkin, no matter how many years I lived in New York.

Rothwax looked good even though he was a bit chubbier, a bit balder, and he still wore a business suit from a bygone era.

"It has been awhile," he said.

"Too long," I noted.

"You still hanging out with that stage designer?"

"On and off," I said. Rothwax had never liked Tony Basillio, and the feeling was mutual.

He cocked his head and gave me one of those hard looks. "You're aging well, Cat Woman."

The very definition of a backhanded compliment, wasn't it? But I did not take offense. I knew he meant well. "Thank you, Detective Rothwax. I go to European spas regularly to keep my complexion glowing."

He laughed in appreciation. "And acting?" he asked. "You still do that too?"

"Yes."

"I always keep an eye out for you."

I wasn't following him. "You mean at the theater?"

"Nah. I never go to the theater. The last time I went was when I was twelve years old. My father took me to Flatbush Avenue in Brooklyn to see *Brigadoon*. I meant that I look for your name in the newspapers. You know. To see if Alice Nestleton, star of stage and screen, was asked to leave a posh joint in the Village because of her inebriated behavior."

"I was never famous enough to get into the gossip columns. Besides, you know I never drink to excess."

"But you are working?"

"It's been a bad year, to be honest."

He made a face. "If you're so good, Cat Woman—and everyone always said you were—how come these directors and producers aren't lining up to hire you?"

"It's a mystery, isn't it?"

"Wrapped in an enigma."

"And cradled in an artichoke."

We both laughed at my absurd finish to his metaphor. He rummaged around in the top drawer of the desk and finally extracted a dark cigar, which he rolled around on his fingertips and sniffed at but never actually lit.

"Actually," Rothwax said, "I did hear a few things about you."

"Oh?"

"It seems that I was not the last NYPD homicide detective you harassed."

I had an inkling of what he meant. He had probably heard of my brief involvement, romantic and professional, with Aaron Stoner. "Harassment is a serious charge, Rothwax."

"In fact," he said, "I heard you simply can't butt out of what doesn't concern you when—when—how do I put this?" He threw up his hands, unable to think of an apt phrase. Private security work had dulled his tongue apparently.

"How about 'unable to butt out when I get a whiff of death'?" I offered.

"Not bad, Cat Lady, not bad. If you can't get acting work, maybe you ought to try your hand at writing the plays."

"I've thought of it."

"All of this leads me to believe you're not here strictly on a social call. Am I right? Oh, I know you miss me and all, but I just have this nagging twitch on the back of my neck."

"Actually I was going to be sociable a bit longer, Rothwax. I mean, I was going to ask you all kinds of questions about Korean groceries and the various threats to that industry. And I'd have listened with a fascinated expression on my face. But maybe I ought to just get right to the point."

"That would be nice too."

"I need your help," I said.

He groaned audibly.

Quickly I told him the contours of my predicament: what had happened, what was happening, and what was about to happen if he would help me. He kept shaking his head and rolling his eyes as if he were listening to a fable told by an inebriated sailor.

"So," I finished off, "I want you to accompany me to the home of this woman Annette Vlakos. You don't have to say a word. Just be there with me."

"Look, Cat Woman, I'm not authorized to conduct investigations unless a Korean market gets held up. And even then—"

I interrupted him. "Didn't you hear me? You are just there for support."

"And intimidation?" he added.

"Something like that. But not quite that."

"When is this confrontation supposed to take place?" he asked.

I picked up his phone without asking permission, dialed 411, and got Vlakos's phone number. I called the number. When she picked up, however, I broke the connection and replaced the receiver on its cradle.

"She's at home right now," I reported.

"This is lunatic," Rothwax said.

"I wouldn't say that. Call it a long shot."

"A very long shot," he added, "on a very muddy track."

"Do you have any other suggestions, Detective Rothwax? Other than, of course, just telling my suspicions to the NYPD."

"That's an option," he said, being disingenuous.

"Telling who?" I demanded. "Why should the police listen to me? Holland killed himself. Case closed. And one detective at one uptown precinct is chasing down a bunch of street hoodlums. He never heard of Holland. He has no idea Frank Loeb was a major contributor to a soup kitchen. He knows nothing. No! It's *not* an option, Rothwax. Besides, I'm not here for a lecture in procedure. I need help."

"The whole story is unbelievable."

"So are Santa's reindeer."

"Shame on you, Cat Woman," he said, then shook his head morosely. "Do you remember that song, Cat? It's called 'What Kind of Fool Am I?' "

Before I could answer, he had risen from his desk chair and grabbed a mackinaw from the coatrack. I noticed that he still carried his weapon in a clearly visible holster, just to the left of his belt buckle.

I kept my hand pressed against the buzzer on the iron gate until I heard the inner door opening. Then I released it.

After peering out, Annette Vlakos stepped into the small courtyard, her face grim as death.

As we watched her approach, Rothwax whispered into my ear, sounding positively gleeful, "I don't think she likes you, Cat Woman."

"If it isn't the Queen of Ramifications," Ms. Vlakos said scornfully. "Who is that with you, the Prince of Obtuseness?"

"It's cold out here, Miss Vlakos. May we come in? It's very important."

"Look. I told you the other day. I don't wish to talk to you. I don't know you, and I don't wish to know you. Now go away and leave me alone or I'll call the police."

I could hear Rothwax chuckling behind me.

There was no time to be cute. There was no space to do anything but drop my bombshell now.

"I know that you participated in the murder of Frank Loeb," I said heavily.

Her entire body stiffened, and the color seemed to bleed out of her face. She staggered a bit, backward, and her hand began to pull at one of her plaits.

I had obviously struck a nerve. So I gave the harpoon some slack. "It would be best for you if you talk to me now, Miss Vlakos. Or perhaps you would prefer the police, whom you seem so anxious to call."

"You are mad," she muttered aloud.

"Let us in."

She obeyed, opening the iron door slowly. She led us into her basement apartment as if she were sleepwalking. Up close, I realized she was even taller than I had thought. She towered over both Rothwax and me.

The apartment was actually quite lovely. The wood floors were highly polished, and the pieces of furniture were elegantly displayed, like in a prized dollhouse.

There was a piano in one corner. She pointed to the bench. That was obviously where she wanted us to sit. Like schoolchildren, Rothwax and I shared the undersize seat, shoulder to shoulder. He undid his mackinaw and the suit jacket beneath it. His weapon was clearly visible.

Annette Vlakos stood in the middle of the room. She had regained her composure except for the ceaseless pulling at her braid.

None of us spoke for what seemed like a very long time. On the walls, I noticed, were several lush landscapes, perhaps depicting the south of France, perhaps Greece. It was hard to tell. Music was coming from somewhere—Purcell, I think.

Finally Annette spoke. "Why don't you tell me in a calm and measured way what your complaint is with me?"

"I'd be delighted," I said. "I know that you met Frank Loeb many years ago at Juilliard. I know that the two of you shared an interest in the flute. I know that you and Will Holland were lovers. I know or at least I presume that Holland found out the identity of the man who gave so much money anonymously to Sustenance House, and then he found out that you knew him also. I know that you and Will Holland conspired to get some of Frank Loeb's money. And you murdered him in the process. Then Will Holland, unhinged by the violence, did violence to himself. I also believe that the murder of Loeb was just greed out of control . . . that you didn't mean to kill him . . . and that if you are forthcoming with answers, you will probably avoid a first-degree murder charge."

She smiled softly at me. Then she did the oddest thing. She just sat down on the floor in the lotus position.

"Did you say Frank Loeb contributed money to Sustenance House, Miss . . . What was the name again?"

"Nestleton. Yes, I did. Eighty-one thousand dollars a year, as you well know. And, as you well know, it was only a portion of his trust fund."

She smiled again. "I knew Frank Loeb for twenty years. He never had a dime."

"Sure," I said caustically.

"Tell me, Miss Nestleton, do you often barge into people's homes with such outlandish accusations?"

"No."

"That's good. Because they really are out-landish, those charges. In fact, they show you to be one of the biggest fools I have ever met."

I gritted my teeth and did not reply. I cast a quick look at Rothwax, who was innocently studying one of the landscapes.

"Now, as painful as it is going to be, Miss Nestleton, I am going to take a minute or so before I throw you and your friend out and show you what a fool you are."

"I'm waiting."

"But first I'm curious about something. Do you know anything about me, really, other than your belief that I'm a kind of ax murderer?"

"No," I admitted.

"Nothing?"

"I've told you what I know. It seems to me that was quite enough."

"I mean, for example, do you know how I make a living? Or am I independently wealthy like you claim Frank was?"

I didn't reply.

"Very well, I'll tell you. I make a living as a grief counselor. That is my profession. Do you know what a grief counselor does?"

"Vaguely."

She looked over at Rothwax. "And you?"

He shook his head no.

"A grief counselor is a professional who treats individuals who have lost loved ones and cannot cope with the loss. The bereaved is usually terribly depressed, affectless, and often suicidal. The treatment phase can occur in the bereaved's home, at the counselor's office, or just about anywhere. That, precisely, was my relationship with Will Holland, you foolish woman. I was his therapist—his grief counselor—on and off for the past few years, since the death of his brother. Will Holland and I lovers? My God, woman! How stupid are you?"

She then leaped up from her cross-legged position on the floor and walked swiftly over to a closet. She pulled out a cardboard carton and probed furiously in it. She soon found an envelope, emptied its contents onto the floor, and selected one item. This she brought over to me and thrust it at me.

"Please . . . inspect it," she ordered.

It was a bank check, canceled. I took it. She had written a check for fifty dollars on last June 18, payable to Frank Loeb.

Annette stood right over me. "So what do you

think? If I had known that Frank was a secret moneybags, would I have given him fifty bucks for the use of his cats?"

"His *cats*?" I asked, startled. "Tiny and Tim?"

"Who else? But here too you are in the dark, aren't you? Tell me, did you ever hear of companion animals?"

"Do you mean seeing eye dogs? Something like that?"

"No. Not that. Those are highly trained animals. Companion animals are simply uncommonly kindly beasts that have a knack with people. They are widely used in mental hospitals, prisons, and old-age homes. Grief counselors employ them too. I certainly do. They are animals who have a God-given ability to bond immediately with a troubled human and enable said human to express love once again. Tiny and Tim are wonderful examples of the breed. I used them for Will Holland, but alas, in his case the cats could do nothing. Nor could anyone else. No one could get through to him anymore. As for Frank Loeb, of course I knew Frank for many years. We went to concerts together. I never knew he had a dime to his name, but I loved him all the same—and his wonderful cats too. Do you realize now how stupid you have been? Do you realize how impossible your scenario is? A profoundly depressed, suicidal man conspiring with his grief counselor to murder a man whose cats she used in her work—and whom she knew only as a poor music student."

She pulled the old check from my hand, ripped it up in a fury, and scattered the pieces over my head. I felt myself growing smaller and smaller. Everything she said made sense now. And the companion cats ... well, that would explain everything, including Tony Basillio's bizarre behavior as of late. They had worked their magic on him too.

"Anything else you want to know?" Annette Vlakos said triumphantly.

I couldn't meet her eyes. I was simply too ashamed.

"Let's get out of here," Rothwax said quietly. He lifted me from the piano stool and led me toward the door.

I heard Ms. Vlakos yell after us. "If you don't believe me, call poor Will's other grief counselor. Her last name is Mizrachi."

Then Rothwax and I were out on the street. "Where can we get a cup of coffee?" he asked.

"I know a place," I said, feeling close to tears. "Gigi's. It isn't far."

My old friend took my arm firmly.

Once inside and seated, Rothwax ordered two cappuccinos and two large glasses of water.

"It's very warm in here," he said, and peeled off his mackinaw and his suit jacket. Then he moved the holster on his belt around so the weapon was not prominent.

About thirty seconds later I started to cry. Oh, it had been a long time since I had cried like that. But it had also been a long time since I had been so ashamed of myself . . . that I had been so bloody wrong about everything.

By the time the coffees were delivered I had cried myself out.

"I'm sorry to be carrying on like this," I apologized to Rothwax.

He shrugged. He slid my cup in front of me. "Win a few, lose a few," he muttered.

I sipped my drink, drawing strength from the delicious brew.

"The way I look at it," Rothwax said, "this is a very minor error. Nobody got hurt. Let's say you just didn't know what the hell you were doing. You took a few pieces of evidence—if you can call them that—and put them together with some of your special Cat Woman glue and made a perfect . . . giraffe. But there ain't no giraffe there."

He paused, wiping his mouth with a cloth napkin to remove the residual foam. Then he sat back expansively.

"You think you just fouled up? Let me tell you about a real foul-up. I was a rookie cop working a patrol car out in Fort Hamilton. You know the neighborhood?"

"Just that it's in Brooklyn."

"Right. On the Brooklyn side of the Verrazano Bridge. A nice middle-class community. It was about this time of year. A lot of Christmas decoration in that neighborhood. Every house seemed to be lit up. Anyway, make it around ten in the evening. We get a call saying there's a mugging in progress only three blocks away from where we are. We tear over there. But we get there too late. A young couple has been held up at gunpoint. Witnesses say the perp was a swarthy, squat man wearing a gray sweatshirt. He was last seen running toward the highway; that's the Belt Parkway around those parts. My partner figures the perp had a car parked near the bridge as a getaway vehicle. All he has to do is drive it over the bridge into Staten Island.

"So my partner and I drive to one of the small parks near the bridge, figuring we can head him off. We park our patrol car and split up, each of us working our way toward the bridge and the highway that abuts it. I remember being able to see the river as I searched. The Hudson was wild that night. I swear to God I saw small white-capped waves. Can you imagine? Waves in the Hudson River.

"Anyway, where was I? Oh, yeah . . ." He paused. "You okay, Cat Woman?"

"I'm fine. What happened?"

"Well, I'm looking and looking, and I don't see anyone at all. I mean, no one is even walking a dog. Then suddenly, out of a clump of shadows and trees, a guy comes running! It's him! The perp! A dark, squat guy in a gray sweatshirt. 'Halt!' I yell. 'Halt!' But he keeps running. I go after him. In those days, Cat Woman, I was really hard . . . in shape . . . well put together. I catch up with the guy, tackle him, take him down. But boy, does he struggle. I finally wallop him on the side of the head with my flashlight. Then I cuff him behind his back, place him under arrest, and read him his rights even though he is now too groggy to know what the hell is going on.

"Then I call to my partner and tell him I got the perp and we're heading back to the patrol car. My partner's waiting for me. The moment I approach with my collar I realize something is wrong. I mean something is very wrong."

He leaned over the table toward me and said in a hushed voice, "Guess what my partner did when we got there."

"Congratulate you?"

"Wrong. He saluted."

"Was that strange?"

"No. Listen. He didn't salute *me*. He was saluting the perp!"

"That certainly is strange."

"Not really. You see, the guy I had tackled and conked on the head and busted was named Ormandy. He was a lieutenant in a homicide division in Brooklyn North. He lived in the neighborhood and was just out for his evening jog."

I laughed for a long time. His story did make me feel better.

"So what are you going to do now?" he asked.

"I don't know."

"You just have to find a few more pieces and

put them all together again. But this time it can't come out looking like a giraffe. . . . Maybe an elephant?"

"Or a mouse," I said wearily. "To be honest, I don't know if I should do anything. I think, as they say, I gave it my best shot, and it fell far, far short."

He nodded in affirmation.

"Aren't you from Ohio originally, Cat Woman?"

"No. Minnesota. I grew up on my grandmother's dairy farm."

"You go home for Christmas?"

"No. There's no one left there."

"Oh. Probably too cold there anyway."

"Probably."

"What kind of Christmas dinner would your grandma make?"

That was an odd question, I thought. It reminded me of the hundreds of elaborate goose dinners that the poor people of Sustenance House wouldn't be having this year. Because Frank Loeb was dead. But I did my best to answer Rothwax's question.

"We never had anything too exotic," I said. "Her staple meals all year were either chicken or meat loaf. On holidays she just made both. The only thing she really did special for Christmas was a whole lot of stewed fruit. Wait—there were also roasted sweet potatoes with the chicken and meat loaf. And then we often went to a neighboring farm for Christmas dinner. They always made lamb."

I realized I was beginning to wander. I shut up. Rothwax drained his cup. "It's time for me to get back to the office," he declared.

"Thanks for helping me out."

"Anytime. But not soon," he replied, laughing. And then he was gone, leaving a ten-dollar bill under his cup.

I sat there for about twenty minutes longer and then walked home slowly, with a slight case of chills.

It was forty minutes past the noon hour when I arrived at my loft.

Three calls had come in.

When I saw the flashing lights of the answering machine, I had the distinct feeling that while yes, I had made a terrible error in my accusation of Annette Vlakos, that was all water under the bridge.

I felt sure that these calls would be professional

ones. A cat-sitting assignment. A part. Something like that.

Wishful thinking. I was wrong.

The first call was from Tony. He would be staying another day or two in New Haven. He missed me "like mad." And please keep taking special care of the twins.

The second message was from Nora. In the background one could hear running water, dishes clinking, and pots and pans being slammed around. Obviously she was using the wall phone in the kitchen of the bistro. Hers was a short message too. She wanted to know the latest developments in "the case of the three thousand goose dinners heist," as she laughingly called it. She asked me to call her back immediately if there were any other bartenders who had to be flirted with. I was finding little humor in her message.

Jack Rugow was the third caller. "Alice, baby, honey, beauty queen, thespian beyond compare . . . How do you like that for a start?

"I need another favor. Half our volunteer staff seems to have vanished overnight. Can you do one more tour on the soup line with your magic ladle? Tonight? I need you to be here around five, okay?

"Look. I know you've already given a lot of time and effort to Sustenance House, and believe me, we're grateful. Just one more time, Alice. Please?"

He laughed then. "This ain't just your run-of-the-mill callback. If you want the part, all you have to do is show up."

That was it. I caught a glimpse of that infernal candy cane on the table. It was just a piece of candy—wasn't it?

Well, all right, I thought. Why not help them out one more time? And then sayonara to soup ladles and peppermint candy, murder investigations, weird philanthropists, and all the rest of those Yuletide spiderwebs.

I arrived at Sustenance House a few minutes past five. The serving line was being set up. I didn't see Jack, but I waved hello to Ishmael Rood and Samuel Mortimer and David Devries, conversing near the coffee urns. Raya Lambert, the hat designer, was swabbing out one of the urns with a huge brush. Not one of them returned my greeting.

The place was jammed with people because it had gotten colder and early arrivals for the meal were allowed to wait inside.

Two men, derelict in appearance, wheeled out the huge soup tureen and placed it on the table. The ladle hung off one handle of the serving dish. The two men walked away, and I lifted the heavy lid of the tureen. Ah. Mushroom barley soup. Thick and heady.

I stepped behind the tureen, picked up the ladle, and got ready for all comers. For some reason, at that moment I had a brief but pleasurable fantasy that all this was just a play being performed on the London stage, about an angel of mercy in World War I.

Then I saw Jack Rugow across the room beckoning urgently to me. I replaced the ladle, put the lid back on the tureen, and walked over to him.

I was expecting him to thank me for showing up as requested. I had a self-effacing little speech accepting his thanks all prepared.

But he didn't say a word; he merely led me into the small room with the unused stage, flicked on the light, and slammed the door shut with such ferocity that I nearly jumped out of my skin.

When he turned toward me, his face was as frightening as the sound of the door slamming. "Do you really need money that bad, Alice?"

I hadn't the vaguest idea what he was talking about.

"We all know why you're here now," he said tauntingly.

"I'm here to ladle soup, Jack. Because that's what you asked me to do."

"Soup!" He laughed in an ugly manner. "Very funny, Alice."

Once again I was shocked into silence.

"It's all over, Alice. You can drop the act now, sweetheart. We know what you've been doing now. And I must say it's about the sleaziest piece of . . . sleaze I've come across in a long time."

I tried very hard not to lose my temper. "I don't know what you're talking about, Jack. But if you're going to insult me, I'll just get my things and leave right now."

"Oh, yes, you do that. Go ahead. Get out! No one wants to see you here ever again. Least of all me."

"You are being a complete ass, Jack."

"Oh, really? Look, you. A reporter from the *New York Post* called this afternoon. He told us what's happening. How you're trying to peddle an exposé of Sustenance House, telling all sorts of lies about us. Oh, he said he couldn't reveal his source, but he dropped enough hints for us to realize that it was you. That's why I asked you to come down here to help out tonight. I wanted to tell you off myself in person. I wanted—"

"Shut up!" I cut him off. "You just shut up, Jack. There's not a word of truth in what you're saying."

"I expected you would deny it."

"Who took the call from this reporter?" I asked.

"What does that matter? Why would a reporter lie about something like this? He wants the story. He *wants* to print awful things about us. Nothing would make him happier than to smear us on the front page. But he has to do some checking, give us a chance to deny the charges before he can run with the story. So tell me, Alice, how much did they give you? Five thousand dollars? Ten thousand? Sure, that's a lot of money. But don't you know how much human damage will be done if your lies and fantasies sink this place? How can you live with yourself?"

I brushed past him and out of the room, almost ran past the food tables, and headed for the exit.

I was dazed. My stomach was flipping over. A rough hand grabbed me, stopping my progress.

It was one of the homeless men, this one wearing a green beret. His right eye was swollen shut, and his face was filthy.

"Get your hands off me!" I shouted.

"Why don't you wait on line like everyone else, lady?"

I was furious. "Do you think I need to be here? Do I look like a homeless woman to you?" I demanded.

He shrugged and let me go on. I walked through the door and out onto the street, where I began to walk fast. Very fast.

What a debacle.

Someone had set me up. Someone wanted me out of Sustenance House, and he or she had phoned in the fake story to the paper. Or maybe someone just called Sustenance House and falsely claimed to be a reporter from the *Post*.

It didn't matter. Jack and probably everyone else had bought the lie.

Was it the same person who had sent me the candy cane?

Was I being followed? Watched?

What were they afraid of? What did they think I knew?

Why was I dangerous now?

I had been totally wrong about Annette Vlakos and my theory of a murderous triangle involving her, Will Holland, and Frank Loeb.

I kept walking downtown. Faster and faster. Keep moving, Alice. Get away from that place. It's time to break off the connections. Christmas is coming. End the obsession. Buy a tree. Buy gifts. Pray for peace of the realm. Get some work. No more Sustenance House!

A Salvation Army Santa suddenly loomed up in front of me, shaking his bell under my nose. It snapped me out of my state. I realized I had walked almost thirty blocks downtown. I was now on the corner of Thirty-fourth Street and Second Avenue.

It was getting colder and colder, the wind almost cruel.

I thought: Why not take care of my cat-sitting duties with Tiny and Tim before I go home? It made sense, and I was only eight blocks away from them now.

I threw all the coins I had in my pocket into the Salvation Army pail, then headed toward Tony's apartment. Too late I realized I had flung tokens into the pail along with the money. Alice, you are falling apart.

T and T were waiting for me, seated together near the telephone table. "Hello, catties," I said. "I hear you hire out as nursemaids. Take a good look, ladies. I'm your new patient. I made a fool of myself this morning. And Jack made a fool of me this evening. I really need some companionship."

They regarded me quizzically.

I filled their food dishes and then sat down on the sofa, contemplating my situation—angry, confused, alone.

They ate daintily and began their tag team match of affection. Now that I knew what they were doing, I was even more attuned to their style.

What had Annette Vlakos said? That companion animals had an inborn gift. They were able to break through the disabling grief of the mourner.

Tiny jumped up on the back of the sofa and placed her tiny nose against my neck, as if assuring me that things would be fine.

It was all too much. I grabbed her and kissed her and hugged her and told her how sorry I was that Frank Loeb was dead and said I understood how much she must miss him.

Then Tim hopped up on the sofa beside me as if evaluating the situation.

I let Tiny down. Tim stared at me. I stared back. I started to laugh—a joyful laugh. These wondrous creatures were worth their weight in gold. I realized that I had been pulled out of a very ugly mood or rather seduced out of it. I felt calm and lighthearted.

I closed my eyes and hummed a little. I even giggled. Would the magic that these two little angels possessed work on me as dramatically as it had worked on Tony?

Would I go out and paint pictures on the nearest wall?

Or would I go mad with poinsettias?

Would some kind of wild love overwhelm me?

Was I finally going to be totally, unqualifiedly, absolutely happy for a measurable span of time?

Tiny returned to her bowl of food and resumed her little repast. Perhaps she had become bored with me. After all, I wasn't one of her usual patients, almost comatose with grief after the loss of a loved one.

It was time, I realized, to go. There were my own cats to think of, to feed.

I thanked Tiny and Tim for their expert solicitude, congratulated them on their ability to work even when they themselves were now mourning and needed a home.

Once on the street again I recalled that all my coins and tokens were now in a Salvation Army collection pail. So I walked to Twenty-third and Park, purchased a single token in the subway, walked back upstairs, and took the Twenty-third Street crosstown bus to Eighth Avenue.

Then I headed downtown on foot. The wind had abated. The stores were still open. The restaurants were beginning to serve dinner. The street trees were bedecked and blinking Christmas lights.

Once south of Fourteenth Street, where Eighth Avenue becomes Hudson Street, I slowed down. This was my neighborhood. All the stores were familiar to me . . . and their windows: the fancy new boutique restaurants, the old bars, the antique stores and the stationers, the luncheonettes and the liquor stores. All of them were, in a sense, precious to me. I am, have always been, and always will be a pathological window-shopper, no matter the season. It is the curse of farm girls in the big city.

Was there something I needed for the loft? It seemed so, but I couldn't identify it. Not cat food.

Not cleaning supplies. Not paper goods. Not bread. What?

Well, if I couldn't think of it, I couldn't purchase it. And it probably wasn't all that crucial. Too bad, I thought, that those feline sisters could mute disabling feelings but couldn't do a thing for memory loss.

The crowds on Hudson thinned dramatically as I passed Christopher Street. I would be at home shortly.

Crossing Barrow Street, I saw the small grocery store on the other side of Hudson. Hot soup? Yes! A container of hot chicken and rice soup to take home would be nice. I crossed over, went inside, and got the soup. They had raised the price to two dollars. Astonishing.

Then I walked to Morton Street and waited for the light to cross back. The container, even through the bag, was hot and comforting to my hands.

Had they remembered the crackers? I opened the bag to check. Yes. The crackers were there.

The light changed. I started to cross. Suddenly I realized I wasn't alone. I turned. Yes. A young Hispanic man was crossing the street with me.

He was wearing one of those Arab-style scarves: a very handsome boy.

I moved away from him instinctively.

Then it happened!

He reached across, grabbed the strap of my shoulder bag, and yanked.

I screamed and stumbled. I tried to hold on, but he was too strong. He ripped the bag away and started to run. I recovered and went after him, shouting as I ran. I have no idea what I was saying.

People began running out of stores toward me. The lady from the liquor store on Hudson reached me first, followed by two of her customers. I was on the west side of Hudson now, my strength suddenly gone.

I held onto a parking meter. The boy had run west on Morton and vanished into the night with my bag.

Soon there was a crowd around me. They consoled me. They offered me coffee, cigarettes, a call to the police. I refused them all. I wanted to go home. I didn't want to cry in front of them.

"At least you weren't hurt," said one man. He was right. I wasn't hurt, except for a bruised shoulder. But the suddenness of it, the sheer indignity of it all, kept washing over me. I started to shake. It had been the worst day of my life.

"Breathe deep, keep breathing," said a young woman in a huge floppy hat.

I followed her instructions, and soon my strength returned. I thanked them all for their solicitude. When under stress, I become very polite.

"I'll be fine," I said. "I'm only a few blocks from home."

I stared ruefully backward. In the middle of Hudson Street, squashed by a van, lay the remains of my soup and crackers.

I walked home slowly, along the buildings, fearful that I would need to hold onto something, suddenly.

When I reached my loft building, I fumbled with my keys, realizing how lucky it was that I never keep them in my bag. As I was fumbling, I saw *it*.

At first I could not believe my eyes. My shoulder bag was propped up against the outside door of the building, just sitting there, innocently.

Was it some kind of ruse or trick? I looked around furtively. The street was empty.

How had the mugger known where I lived?

He must have gone through the purse immediately, found my address, taken what he wanted, and given me back the rest.

A kind purse snatcher? A gentleman thief? Was that it? Well, something had to go my way, sooner or later.

But what had he taken? Just the cash? There hadn't been much.

Maybe he hadn't taken my last functioning credit card. Maybe he hadn't taken my driver's license.

I was hoping against hope.

I grabbed the bag and ran upstairs. I ignored the cats and threw the bag on the table. I shook off my coat, then opened the bag and dumped all the contents out.

I found the wallet quickly.

He had taken nothing! Not even the cash!

Something else was strange. Something had come out of the bag that I had never put into it.

It was a thick stack of paper slips fastened with several rubber bands.

I bent over closer—to examine it.

"Oh, no!" I cried out and then turned away from the table. I didn't want to deal with this now. I just *couldn't*.

Chapter 7

One hot bath, two hard-boiled eggs, and ten hours of sleep later I returned to confront the object that had fallen out of my bag.

I sat down. I removed the rubber bands. And I counted $45,500 worth of blank post office and bank money orders—in denominations of $700 and $1,000 for the most part.

It was even more astonishing in the morning. I could tell by the dates on the postal money orders that they had been purchased between the fifteenth and the twenty-fifth of November.

Were these the money orders Frank Loeb had purchased in order to make his annual gift to Sustenance House, the ones that had never been sent because he was murdered?

Probably.

But why would anyone stage a mugging to get them to me?

It dawned on me that now there were two people playing with Alice Nestleton.

One was trying to hurt me—witness the lie of the newspaper exposé. This person wanted me away from the mess—far away.

But someone else was in the game. This was the person who had sent me the candy cane and led me to the Siamese cats.

This person seemed to need my help, to want me to get involved.

But which of them had sent me the money, and why?

And what was I to do with $45,500 worth of untraceable money orders? As good as cash.

To whom did it belong?

Who should I give it to? Sustenance House? The estate of Frank Loeb?

Who should I report it to? The police? David Devries? Jack Rugow? Who?

Tony would say, "Let's blow it all on a trip to Paris, London, and Rome. Take me along. You can afford all kinds of cat-sitters now."

No, that wouldn't do.

I walked to the window. The poinsettias were

fiercely blooming in the morning sun—aggressive, mesmerizing red. Or was it vermilion?

Bushy was beside one, on a ledge, contemplating chewing again. Pancho was stalking something by the closet door. His poor little half tail was moving back and forth in anticipation of finding something. Good luck, old gray cat.

I walked back to the table and hefted the money orders in my hand.

Yesterday, before the "mugging," I had accepted the fact that my investigative services at Sustenance House were no longer wanted or needed. Now I had been thrust back into the center of it—for reasons unknown, by persons unknown. Now I had to identify one of those persons: either the one who had tried to repel me or the one who had tried to engage me.

For the first time I felt an incredible sense of urgency, as if the money on my table now put me at risk. In more ways than one.

How could I flush them out? Either one of them.

I had to think, improvise. I had to clarify, reduce, shake out.

So I made myself some peppermint tea and toast. I curled up on the sofa with my repast.

The key, I knew, was Frank Loeb. It was time to forget Will Holland. Loeb would have to be the bait. But he was, like John Brown, buried in his grave.

His money? In a trust fund.

The donation that had never arrived? I had at least half of it.

What was left of that eccentric recluse's life that could entice anyone? A flute? Probably that was all: an instrument that he seemed to have abandoned and that was probably worthless.

An old flute in an old case. Sad.

I sat up so suddenly that I knocked the peppermint tea over and the cup shattered on the floor.

Pancho went bananas. Bushy strolled over leisurely to evaluate the damage.

"An old flute in an old case," I whispered to my Maine coon.

Oh, yes!

I stood up. It was worth a shot. The most pathetic little wildflower always seems to attract the most aggressive pollen gatherers.

But I needed a companion to set this trap. A companion, if not a friend. Because my prospective accompanist was someone considerably less friendly than Detective Rothwax.

* * *

"I cannot believe your gall. I simply can't believe that you are ringing my doorbell again," said Annette Vlakos furiously, standing in the small basement courtyard between her front door and the iron grate.

She calmed down a bit. She folded her arms. "Maybe," she continued, "I should call Bellevue rather than the police."

"Please," I urged through the grate, "I need your help! I'm sorry for what happened the other day. I'm sorry about those ridiculous accusations. Sorry and ashamed of myself."

She seemed to be evaluating my sanity. Finally she shrugged and let me in. After all, she was a "grief counselor." She did deal with people in extremis—and I surely was in that state.

The apartment was cold that day; the boiler had conked out, Annette said. She was wearing many sweaters, the top one with a hood. Annette Vlakos looked then like a large suspicious bird of prey. A falcon. And everyone knows that the female of that species is swifter and more deadly.

I didn't equivocate. I wasn't cute. We were standing, facing each other in the middle of the small room.

"Here is what we are facing," I said.

"We? Who is this 'we'? Are you pregnant?"

I laughed. The ice was broken.

Then I told her sequentially everything that had transpired from the moment I received the call from Jack Rugow asking to buy me a drink in the Corner Bistro on Jane Street. I didn't editorialize. Nor did I evaluate or elaborate. I just gave her a descriptive calendar of events.

She listened, intent, her arms folded, swaying slowly from side to side. When I had finished, she said, "That is an incredible story."

"Believe me, it's all true."

"But why are you telling *me*? I already explained that I am out of the loop."

"I know that. I need you to come into the loop."

"Why?"

"Because I know you loved Frank Loeb in your fashion. And I know you want to see his killer brought to justice."

"Of course I do. But I don't know how I can help. You did say the police believe he was murdered by a street gang."

I didn't have time to waste on theory. "Do you know what happened to his flute?" I asked.

"No."

"Neither do I. But he did have one, didn't he?"

"Of course. At least he had one years ago. People tend to hold on to instruments they once played, even if they don't play a note anymore."

"And the flute had a case?"

"Yes."

"And is a flute case large enough to hold respectable sums of money?"

"I suppose so."

"And people develop a sentimental attachment to old instruments?"

"Most certainly."

"You see: money or love," I said.

"What are you talking about?"

"I think someone would want to get hold of Frank Loeb's instrument."

"Why?"

"As I said, for money or love. Someone may think that is where he kept his money. Oh, I know you were unaware of his trust fund. But he had money, believe me. Or someone may have had a relationship with him so intense that the instrument has become a kind of memory, a totem they must have."

"There is a certain logic in what you say,"

Annette Vlakos agreed. "But—and it is a big but—as you said yourself, no one knows where the flute is. Maybe it's still in the apartment. Who knows?"

"We can make believe we have it. After all, you were his music teacher once. Why wouldn't he have entrusted it to you? It makes sense. He lived in a high-crime area."

"So do I," she laughed. "But tell me, Miss Nestleton. Exactly what are you proposing?"

"Do you have a sheet of paper?"

She produced one.

I sat down beside a small table and wrote carefully:

—yuletide memorial for frank loeb—his beautiful flute in its original case will be auctioned shortly. proceeds will go to the barking ark for its cat adoption program. view the instrument between 2–4 p.m. at 211$\frac{1}{2}$ e. 12th street (basement) on december 20 & 21.

—Annette Vlakos

I handed the paper to her. She read it slowly, her eyebrows arching.

"Who is going to get this?" she asked.

"I propose that you bring it to Sustenance

House. Ask to see David Devries, the director, introduce yourself, and give it to him. I am sure he will show it to all the other directors on the board. Then I think you should post a copy of it uptown—in Loeb's building lobby. His neighbor told me a strange man has been prowling about there. Let him see it also, whoever he is."

"You're asking me to do a lot."

"I know. Believe me, I know. And I wouldn't ask if I could think of any other way to proceed."

"Will I be in any danger?"

"I doubt it. I'll wait here with you. The moment someone rings your bell, I'll take over."

Skeptical, she shook her head. "If there is all that money around, someone might come in with guns blazing."

"Then I'll be dead, Annette. May I call you Annette?"

She laughed nervously.

I continued. "Seriously, I think all they'd want to do is inspect the case for hidden money or verify, somehow, that the instrument they are inspecting is indeed Frank Loeb's flute. Of course, they'll never get the chance to do either. The play ends the minute I open the door."

"Who will it be?"

"I haven't the vaguest notion. Five out of the six directors are still alive, and all claim to have no knowledge of or acquaintance with their secretive benefactor. It's one of them, that's for sure. Or two . . . because I have the distinct feeling that two people, at odds with each other, are waging a covert battle."

"Using you as an intermediary," she noted.

"Or as the sponge."

There was a long silence. She played with the paper. She was making up her mind. I said nothing further.

Then she whispered something I didn't catch.

"What?"

"I said, it seems such a whimsical trick to catch such a deadly foe."

"It is, I suppose, whimsical. But believe me, I don't expect someone to knock on your door, demand to see the flute before it's auctioned, and then grandly announce that he or she murdered Frank Loeb. I just want to find out who I am dealing with. Just a face. I need a face."

"What are you going to do with the money?" she asked.

"I don't know yet."

Annette nodded. "You probably aren't aware of

it, but they were both, in their way, the loveliest of men. One died from grief, the other from greed. That is not the way to go, is it, Miss Nestleton?"

"Please call me Alice."

"Well, Alice, you have a coconspirator."

We proceeded to the nuts and bolts.

Late that afternoon, the same afternoon that Annette Vlakos and I became plotters, companions—coconspirators, to use her word—Tony Basillio called. He was still in New Haven.

But he was no longer Saint Anthony of the Poinsettias. Obviously the transforming powers of the companion cats did not last long. They had to be continually reinforced.

In fact, Tony was downright nasty for its being so close to Christmas.

He cursed the job interviewer. He cursed the entire faculty—both academic and janitorial—of the august Yale Drama School. He cursed the city of New Haven. He even came down hard on me, coming up with the outlandish fiction that he wouldn't be in New Haven if it hadn't been for me, that I had been pressuring him to find a steady job.

Then he hinted that he might go out discoing

with a beautiful young acting student he had just met up there.

"The disco is a thing of the past," I noted.

"Not up here, it isn't," he replied.

"Do what you want to do, Tony. I'm neither your chaperone nor your moral adviser."

He began to chuckle. "Do you really think I'm going to start cheating on you again, Swede?"

I didn't answer. I really wasn't up to this kind of conversation at this time. My thoughts were on the "trap" . . . and my thoughts were nervous.

Annette Vlakos had characterized the idea as whimsical. The word was beginning to torment me, much more than Tony's always possible promiscuity.

Why had I acted so hastily? Why hadn't I really thought it out? Why had I just leaped in and pulled Annette Vlakos in with me?

That's the trouble with being an actress. It's hard for other people to resist your conceits. You seem so authentic, so sure, almost hypnotically persuasive when you're really into the part.

Tony's call had sobered me. It was entirely possible that this trap would turn out ineffectual and pathetic. The more I thought about it, the more such an outcome seemed plausible.

I don't like to be embarrassed. And I couldn't afford in this case to play the fool. There was risk all around now—palpable, threatening risk. I stared at my table. The money orders were lying next to that candy cane.

Then Tony asked me to send him some money.

I laughed into the receiver. "You know my bank balance."

"Yeah, I know. Borrow from Nora, and wire it up to me. I'm down to my last thirty-four cents."

I glanced again at the pile of money orders. They seemed so pale, so cold, so still. They were really beginning to unnerve me.

"Tony, what would you say if I told you I had found close to fifty thousand dollars on the subway?"

"In a brown paper bag?"

"Yes."

"On the D train, right?"

"Yes."

"I'd say, bring it to me immediately and I'll take *you* to the disco. In fact, we'll buy the disco."

"Be serious."

"Serious! What do you mean, a serious fantasy?"

"Yes. Not going to Shangri-la in a silver rickshaw."

"All right. Let's see . . . a serious fantasy. If you found almost fifty thousand bucks on the D train, even if you found it in a plastic bag, I would—"

He stopped. There was silence. He was obviously collecting his thoughts.

"I'm waiting," I said.

"Okay. Here goes. I would buy a loft building under the Williamsburg Bridge . . . or in Greenpoint . . . or even the Bronx. We would start a theatrical company. Our first production would be the wildest, most brilliant staging of *Mother Courage* ever mounted. I mean, it would blow your mind. Not set in the Thirty Years War but in Bosnia or Rwanda or the West Bank. And you would be the most provocative Mother Courage ever to pull a wagon across a stage. You would redefine the role. Poor old Brecht would rise up from the grave, so startled by your great performance that he could be heard muttering, 'Is she really from Minnesota?'"

"So that's what you'd do."

"Without question."

"I'll keep it in mind if I'm on the D train."

"You do that. Now let's talk just a few bucks.

Are you going to let your true love go to a disco with only thirty-four cents in his pockets?"

"Do you have a round trip ticket?"

"Yeah."

"Good. When you spend your thirty-four cents, come home."

And that was that.

I held onto the phone, waiting for him to hang up. This was a holdover from childhood. My grandmother had instilled in me the notion that it was impolite to be the first to hang up. One always waited for the other person to disconnect. I thought that habit had long ago been dispensed with, but it seemed, right then, to have been suddenly and inexplicably resurrected. Maybe it had something to do with all that money staring me in the face.

Anyway, Tony didn't hang up.

"You really want to hear the truth?" he asked in an uncommonly low voice.

"I always want that. But what truth are we talking about?"

"The fantasy, what I would really want us to do if you stumbled upon fifty thousand dollars."

"Oh, yes, tell me a true fantasy."

"A small house in the country."

"You're kidding."

"No, honest. A small house with a big kitchen window. And there's a garden behind the house. And you're in the garden all the time. And around us are gentle slopes of trees, a lot of high, elegant oaks. It's the Berkshires, Swede. There are deer and raccoons and a black bear or two and hawks and cardinals and chipmunks. Above all, chipmunks. It has been a long time since I saw a chipmunk. They vanished from the city when I was a kid. Anyway, there you are in the garden with a trowel and a pair of work jeans and a flannel shirt rolled up to the elbows. And your face is all flushed, and you're happy. You're happier than you ever have been in your life. And I spend a lot of time just staring out that one large window . . . at you, at the chipmunks . . . at I don't know what."

That was a mouthful for Basillio. It was an astonishing declaration.

"I had no idea you wanted to live that kind of life, Tony."

"Live and learn," he muttered.

"But tell me, how are we making a living? Selling radishes from my garden?"

"Don't bother me with trivial details. I'm giving you essentials."

"Okay. But, Tony, I come from the country, remember."

"No. You come from Minnesota."

"You mean my grandmother's farm doesn't qualify as 'the country'?"

"I mean, it was a harsh place. I'm talking about a little glade filled with daisies and sunshine, a land of milk and honey."

I smiled at his imagery. This was so unlike him. Maybe the second phase of the companion cats' program was driving the patient mad.

"I'll tell you something else, Swede," he said.

"I'm listening."

"Sooner or later we're going to have to do something like that. Money or no money."

"Something like what?"

"You and me. In solitude. Away from everything and everybody."

"Why?"

"You know why."

"I'm sure I don't, Tony. Look, maybe we can continue this conversation some other time. I'm sorry I brought up the subject of money, money that I never found and don't have." The lie didn't bother me at all. I didn't believe those money orders were mine. And I hadn't *found* them; they'd been sent to me.

"No!" Tony suddenly shouted.

" 'No' what?" I said.

"No, we aren't gonna talk about it later. We're going to talk about it now. I'm talking about love, Alice Nestleton. You remember that, don't you? I'm talking about how, no matter what you and I do, no matter how many times we sleep together, we just can't seem to take that final step."

"What step?"

"I guess you could call it fusion."

"So now you're a nuclear scientist, Tony?"

"You know damn well what I mean."

"I really don't."

"How about living for the other? Or radical camaraderie? Two beings, one love. The embrace until death. How many stupid phrases do you want me to utter? You know what I mean, girlie. You've played Juliet enough times."

Suddenly the conversation had somehow become threatening to me. One day, I knew, I would have to deal with what he was saying. But not now!

"And a place in the country is going to fix us up?" I asked with a laugh.

"Don't laugh at me."

"Come on, Tony. Get hold of yourself."

He fell silent. I waited. My hand on the receiver had a slight tremor.

He finally said in a quiet, accusatory voice: "You have forgotten what love is all about, Swede. It is a tiger at the gate. And if there is no tiger, then you have to go into the wilderness and find one."

"I think maybe you've gone crazy, Basillio. Or are you drunk? First it's the bucolic Berkshires with me floating around in a herb garden. And now you think you're William Blake."

"That's me. William Blake on jingle bell rock. I'm like Prometheus. With fifty thousand dollars' worth of sugarplums dancing in my head."

"You're mixing up all kinds of images, Tony. Believe me, the money is make-believe."

"Don't I know it! Love you." And he hung up.

'Tis the season, I thought, for all kinds of jollities.

Nora, a bit manic, called me about an hour later.

"I am going to have some red meat, Alice. I

need red meat. And I want to be served. I'm going to take a cab downtown in two hours, pick
you up, and buy you dinner at Hot Hand Luke."

"What is that?"

"A funky little Southern-style restaurant near
Gramercy Park. I hear they have the best mashed
potatoes, the second-best collards, the third-best
coleslaw, and the fourth-best ten-dollar hamburger in Manhattan."

I was dazzled. But Nora likes to eat in "hip,
funky places," as she calls them. She was trained
in haute cuisine in France after she gave up the
stage, and her Pal Joey bistro serves a basic Conti-
nental menu with a heavy dose of Americana like
Yankee pot roast. Yet when she eats out, which is
often, she ends up in the strangest places. Eating
out for her has to be an adventure. "Or why go?"
she would say.

I accepted her offer. A time was set when I
would meet her downstairs.

In the interim I called Annette Vlakos. She had
performed brilliantly. Devries had the notice. "He
was polite but a bit uninterested," she said.

And she had scotch-taped a copy of the notice
in Frank Loeb's building. "I hadn't been there in

years. We always used to meet elsewhere when we went to concerts," she said.

I told her I would be at her place tomorrow at noon to begin the vigil. She seemed anxious now to get the whole thing over with, as if she, like me, were having second thoughts.

"I feel like a schoolgirl," she declared. That was not good.

Anyway, I hung up and went to feed those sisters of mercy Tiny and Tim. As usual, after I had filled their dishes—it was chicken and liver this time—I sat down on the sofa and waited to be "companioned." As usual, they performed nobly, but this time I had the peculiar desire to speak to them. Now, I often speak to Bushy and Pancho, but it's usually a rather primitive conversation.

With Tim and Tiny, that late afternoon, I actually asked direct, pointed questions. Can you believe it! Worse, I had the feeling they were, in their fashion, answering me.

Whoa! I thought. It is time to go.

Nora and her cab arrived on time, but we had to abandon the vehicle shortly afterward. There was just too much traffic. We completed the journey to Hot Hand Luke on foot.

"Any joint with a name this stupid," Nora said, "has to serve good food."

"Maybe they just serve hard-boiled eggs," I suggested, remembering that scene from the movie *Cool Hand Luke* in which convict Paul Newman eats what seems like hundreds of hard-boiled eggs to win a bet.

"That isn't funny, Alice. And I want only funny talk tonight. I'm not interested in murder, men, or misery of any kind."

We walked into Hot Hand Luke. Now this is whimsical, I thought, as we sat down at a booth that seemed to have been zealously aged, splintered, and dulled.

Everything in the small restaurant—from the splintered wooden door with a loose handle to the bar with wobbly mismatched stools to the ancient and long-disabled vending machines (they had once dispensed plastic combs, hard candy, beef jerky, etc.)—had been placed there in an attempt to capture the mood of a down-and-out roadhouse somewhere south of Gadsden, Alabama, circa 1961.

It was amazing that the place had opened only two blocks from the still elegant Gramercy Park.

But I suppose even those with keys to that private park craved some kind of phony nostalgia.

The music, relentlessly rockabilly, was from a tape deck regulated by the bartender. Old jukeboxes were in each corner of the dining room, and there were smaller versions on the table of each booth, but they all seemed inoperative.

"Red meat," Nora counseled as she refused a scruffy menu offered by a charming young waitress dressed in flannel shirt and torn jeans.

We both ordered burgers with mashed potatoes and coleslaw and collard greens. Medium rare for me, rare for Nora.

"The collards are not part of the burger plate," the waitress said. I wondered if her name actually was Laverne, as the stitching on her shirt read, or if she was in truth a young Tiffany, an Ashley, or an Amber.

"How much for the collards as a side order?" Nora asked.

"Three dollars."

"A bit steep," Nora noted critically. But of course she did order the sides, one for me and one for her.

Then she asked for two bottles of a murkily dark beer called Dixie Voodoo.

"Well, Alice, what do you think of the place?" she asked, leaning toward me and sweeping her eyes along the walls, ceiling, accouterments.

"It's okay."

"A bit overdone, wouldn't you say?"

"I'd say this beer is a bit overdone, Nora." I grimaced as I took a taste of Dixie Voodoo.

"It's good for you, Alice. It's time you took a break from health food."

"Health food? With Tony around? You must be kidding."

"Besides, thick beer is a kind of health food. It was considered medicinal in the Middle Ages."

Five minutes later the burgers arrived.

"A lovely presentation," said Nora.

Indeed it was. The burger itself lay on one half of a sourdough roll. Finely shredded lettuce and two very thin slices of ripe tomato lay on the other half.

The mashed potatoes were southeast of the meat, and northwest on the plate was a small tub of coleslaw. The collards were served in a separate monkey dish.

We commenced our meal with different tactics. I used the traditional approach—dumping the shredded lettuce, joining the two buns over the patty—and picked up the burger with both hands. Nora used a fork and knife, as if she were eating a lamb chop.

The moment I took my first bite I realized this was a superior burger. I mean, it was delicious! A rich, deep tang, like steak.

I took two more bites before putting the burger down and then ate some potatoes and then a forkful of the cole slaw. Equally delicious.

I then took another, larger bite of the hamburger. I was ecstatic, and I am not usually a burger person. Maybe, I thought, it's all the tension combined with the Christmas sleigh ride. Maybe one just needs red meat at certain times.

"You look like you're enjoying yourself," Nora said.

"This burger is so good!" I replied.

"Really?"

The way she said, "Really?" gave me pause.

"What's the matter, Nora? Isn't yours good?"

"Oh . . . well, yes. It's a good-tasting burger. . . ."

She put down her knife and fork and repeated: "A good-tasting burger."

A minute later she called the waitress over. The girl signaled that she'd come soon. Nora picked up her fork and began lightly, but aggressively, to beat it against the side of the plate.

"Nora, what are you doing? What's the matter?"

"Do I look unhappy?"

"Let's trade burgers," I suggested. "Or just take the rest of mine. I've had enough."

She set the fork down then. "My burger, Alice, tastes exactly the same as yours. Believe me."

"Then what's bothering you? I can tell when you're stewing. In fact you're just about ready to boil over."

She gave out with a big sigh.

"Sometimes, Miss Alice, you are very naive. Do you know that? I mean, you're smart, very smart. And you know the score, as they say. And you know a whole lot about a whole lot. But man, oh, man, can you play the country bumpkin sometimes."

"Is that what I'm doing? Now?"

I was completely bewildered. Just then the waitress arrived.

"May I see the menu again?" Nora asked crisply.

The waitress handed it over and started to walk away.

"Just a minute!" Nora barked, causing the young woman to freeze in her tracks.

In a loud voice Nora addressed me: "Alice, please read the description of the burger on this menu." She handed the oversize card to me. "Read it out loud," she ordered me.

Abashed, I complied. "Sixteen scrumptious ounces of Black Angus burger cooked to your instructions," I stammered, "served with 'taters' and 'slaw.'"

"Thank you," she said through tight teeth, then glared up at the waitress.

"So?" the waitress said defiantly. The girl was obviously beginning to lose patience with her customer.

Nora tapped the thick mound of meat again with that damn fork. "Young woman," she said, "the description on the menu clearly implies this is an all-chopped-steak burger. It specifically says 'Black Angus' burger."

"Yeah. So what?"

"There is *pork* in this meat! That's what!"

"Really?" the girl said, her eyes suddenly darting around the room nervously. "Are you sure?"

In reply, Nora forked a piece of the meat, lifted

it from the plate, and shoved it under the girl's nose. "Here," she said, "taste it."

"Oh, no—I—I mean, no, thanks . . . I mean, I'm just a waitress."

"Yes, and I am just a customer," Nora said, now furious. "At least I *was* a customer."

With that, she stood up, gathered her things, and stormed out. I had no option but to follow.

Once we were out on the sidewalk, Nora calmed down quickly. "It's not that I object to a little pork sausage in a burger as filler," she said. "In fact it livens up the meat. But I don't like cheap subterfuge. After all, I am a restaurateur. Let's find someplace else to eat."

And so we did. At the bar of a spanking new bistro a couple of blocks off the main strip of trendy eateries.

But the meal was not satisfying for either of us, because by that time—country bumpkin notwithstanding—I was a grumpy dinner companion.

Tomorrow was intruding on me. The case of the pork-laced burger seemed to portend trouble.

Chapter 8

"What if no one shows up?" she asked.

We were seated across a tiny table on old high-backed chairs in the basement apartment on Twelfth Street.

"Then no one shows up."

Annette Vlakos was nervous, unsure, overwrought. She was now having more second thoughts than that burger had pork. It was now one-thirty; we had been sitting like that since noon.

"Or what if someone totally unknown shows up? Suppose that Devries posted it and someone saw it and is coming just out of curiosity. Maybe a volunteer who helps out at Sustenance House—some musician, for example. Maybe an old derelict saw the notice, and he thinks he can try and steal the instrument and pawn it."

"I'll deal with the possibilities as they present themselves," I assured her.

"Do you think I should take my own flute out of the closet and put it out in plain view?"

"No, I don't think that's necessary, Annette."

"Anyway, you made a very bad error when you wrote that notice," she said gravely.

"What error?"

"You didn't mention the name of the auction house. That's always mentioned. In fact, the 'viewing' usually takes place there."

I nodded. "You're right. But it's too late for that now."

The heat had come on again, and the radiators were hissing. My, how they hissed!

"Do you want something to eat, Alice?"

"No, thanks."

"But maybe we *should* eat something."

"Thank you very much, but I'm not hungry."

"Well, I certainly should get some food down."

All I could do was nod. This woman was losing her nerve, I realized. It was time to change the subject, to bring her back to her professional discipline.

"You know, I've been spending a lot of time with Tiny and Tim. They are remarkable cats."

She sat up straight and looked at me as if I had uttered a ridiculous statement. Then she said, "Well, of course they're wonderful. They're companion animals. But no different from a dozen others I've known in the past. Dogs are usually better, though it depends on the subject."

"How do you mean?"

"Let us assume a couple has been married for twenty years. They have always had a dog in the household. Then the wife dies suddenly. The husband slips into a dangerous, suicidal depression. You would think that if a companion animal could be obtained for him, that animal should be a dog."

"It makes sense," I said.

"But in fact it doesn't work that way. It is better to have an animal that the husband has absolutely no experience with. A dog, in this case, might trigger memories that would send him deeper into his grief. A cat, on the other hand, if said cat had the 'companion' gift, might be therapeutic."

"There's another question about so-called companion animals that puzzles me," I said. "Do you use them for—"

The doorbell rang, interrupting me. The sound, objectively slight, was subjectively like a clap of thunder.

I shut up.

We both leaned forward, like puppets. The intrusion was frightening.

"Could it be a delivery of some sort?" I asked in a whisper.

She shook her head no.

"Maybe a neighbor?"

"No! No!" Annette was also speaking in an urgent whisper. "It's too early. It's not yet two o'clock. Oh . . . this is very bad."

I looked around the small apartment, searching for a weapon—any kind of weapon. I was on the edge of panic.

Stop this nonsense, I told myself. Pull yourself together, Cat Woman. There is no danger.

I stood up. I took a deep breath. "You stay just where you are!" I ordered Annette.

I walked stiffly toward the door. The bell rang again . . . and then again. The sound was becoming softer.

Turning the knob, I pushed the door open and stepped into the courtyard.

The winter sun was dazzlingly bright. A bundled figure stood on the other side of the iron gate. There was something so endearing about the figure that I burst into laughter.

Her features came into focus. We stared uncomprehendingly at each other, the visitor and I. It was Mrs. Boyle, Frank Loeb's neighbor.

"How nice to see you again," I said. "Come on in out of the cold."

She didn't utter a word in response. She merely turned and began to hurry away, as fast as her aged body could move.

"Mrs. Boyle!" I called out. "Just a moment!"

I pushed against the iron fence. It would not budge.

I began shouting for Annette then.

She rushed out a few seconds later and opened the gate for me. I began to run after the old lady, but I didn't have to run very far.

She had half collapsed only twenty yards west and was holding onto an old picket fence surrounding a sweet little front yard.

"Please, Mrs. Boyle, don't run anymore. There's nothing to be afraid of."

She still had not spoken. I saw that she was

now crying. I took her arm and led her slowly back to Annette Vlakos's apartment.

A deep mug of hot tea revived the old woman. After each sip she took off a layer of clothing.

"Did you see the notice that was posted in your lobby, Mrs. Boyle—about Frank's flute? Is that why you're here?" I asked gently.

She stared down into her teacup. For the first time since I opened the door and saw her, I felt a sense of suspicion and dread.

But how could this old lady be the beast in the jungle?

We sat in silence for a long time. Finally she finished her tea. "I must go," she announced.

"Before you do that, Mrs. Boyle," I said firmly, "tell me why you came here."

She threw up her hands in surrender. "To see it," she said.

"The flute?"

"Yes, yes."

"Why?"

"Because it just . . . couldn't be. What's on that sign, that flyer. It just can't be. *I* have his flute. He always kept it in my apartment because he was out of his own apartment most of the time. And there had been so many break-ins, you see."

"You never mentioned that to me when I came to see you, Mrs. Boyle," I said, my tone accusatory. Annette gave me a "stop picking on that sweet old lady" look. I did my best to ignore it.

"Why did you run when you saw me, Mrs. Boyle?" I went on.

"I don't know, dearie. Seeing you again just gave me a scare."

"You're not making any sense, Mrs. Boyle."

"Oh, I'm tired! I have to go. My cat will be missing me. She isn't well, you know."

Annette began helping Mrs. Boyle with her things.

My mind was racing as I watched her struggle into her garments.

I couldn't let her leave. She had taken the bait in the trap. I could not let her go until I made some sense out of all this.

Mrs. Boyle had come to inspect the flute and its carrying case. Why?

What was the bait? Love or money?

Oh, my God! Money! That was it.

The realization staggered me.

If this woman had Frank Loeb's flute and case, she might have— I yanked the sweater out of Annette Vlakos's hand just as she was helping Mrs. Boyle with the many buttons.

She shrank back, regarding me as if I were insane.

"You sent that money to me, didn't you?" I shouted at Mrs. Boyle.

She turned away.

My heart was thumping wildly. "You hired a kid from the neighborhood to fake a mugging and put those money orders into my bag, didn't you? Didn't you, Mrs. Boyle?"

She began to cry.

I shook her arm. "Tell me the truth!"

She sank back into her chair then, and began to bob her head up and down. "I knew it was there," she said through the tears. "I just found it in the case after he died. All those money orders, made out to nobody. I didn't know what to do. Would he have wanted me to have the money? Did he leave the money there on purpose? Please . . . I—I didn't do anything wrong. I didn't steal anything."

"But why did you give it to me?"

"I thought maybe, I don't know, maybe *half* could go to charity. Don't you see? Maybe half for me and my darling Augusta and half for charity. I figured you would know who he used to donate it to."

"You came here today, Mrs. Boyle, because you thought there might have been two flutes. Isn't that it? And perhaps this one had money orders in the case too. Isn't that true?"

"Yes, all right, I did. But I meant no harm. I just wanted to *see*. Oh, please, let me leave."

"Did he leave Tiny and Tim with you as well?"

"No! Believe me, he didn't. They took the cats."

"They? Who do you mean by 'they,' Mrs. Boyle?"

She seemed to freeze, and her eyes grew wild. She began to look around desperately as if searching for an escape route. I hated knowing that I was the one causing her terror and panic.

I knelt beside her. "Listen to me, Mrs. Boyle. Do you know who murdered Frank Loeb? Believe me, nothing will happen to you if you tell the truth. You haven't done anything wrong."

"It wasn't the gang," she said at last.

"Who, then?"

"A man and a woman. I didn't see the man. I saw her—just for a second. There was a lot of shouting. I'd never heard Frank shout like that. I was frightened, so frightened. I never told the police about it. I—I heard his scream ... Frank's scream ... and that funny sound. Like a ball bouncing down the stairs."

"The woman," I said. "Can you tell me anything about her?"

"Only her hair, dearie. It was all frazzled and frizzled."

I stood suddenly, ramrod straight.

"What is it?" an anxious Annette asked. "Why do you look like that, Alice? You're scaring me."

"I know who the woman was," I said. "Yes. I'm sure of it."

"The woman with frizzy hair?"

"That's right. Her name is Daisy. I forget her last name. She's a recovering addict who lives at Sustenance House. She works there."

"And do you know who the man with her was?"

"No. Let's put Mrs. Boyle in a cab and get her home."

"Good idea. The poor woman has had enough for one day."

Annette took Mrs. Boyle outside and hailed a taxi. When she returned to the apartment, we both sat down again, primly, on the facing high-backed chairs. The room had become oppressive, full of menace. It was as if I was Hansel or Gretel and the gingerbread house was closing in on me.

"So our scheme was a success," Annette said.

"In a way."

"What do you mean? What better result could you have expected? Now you know at least one of the individuals who participated in the murder of Frank Loeb."

"I'm not complaining," I replied. "It's just that suddenly I have a rearranged cast of characters to deal with. The understudy is shifting to the lead, and vice versa. More important, I know now the solution is deep inside the physical space of Sustenance House."

"What are you going to do?"

"I don't really know."

"Whatever you do, you'd better do it fast."

"I am aware of that."

"How are you going to get back in there now that you're persona non grata, you know, because of the fake newspaper thing, the story they think you tried to sell about them."

"It will be difficult," I conceded.

"Would you want me to go there for you? I could volunteer for the feeding line."

Annette Vlakos was becoming positively aggressive after her very tentative start in the field of criminal investigation.

"Maybe," she continued, "the atmosphere is just too poisonous for you to go back there. It could be dangerous for you."

I laughed. "It *was* poisonous. As I was being shown the door, a homeless man thought I was trying to barge ahead of him on the food line."

"You mean he thought you were homeless too?"

"Exactly."

"That is incredible. You look a million miles from homelessness, Alice."

"I suppose I do," I replied.

"He must have been drunk."

"Many of them are."

"What did you say to him? How did you respond?"

"I think I just shouted at him because he was mauling me, grabbing my arm."

"Actually it is kind of amusing."

"Now it is, yes. At the time, no."

"Did you ever think what you would do if circumstances made you homeless?"

It was immediately after she asked that question of me that I realized Annette Vlakos had led me exactly to the place I had to be.

Chapter 9

The makeover took only an hour.

It would have taken much longer had it not been for the able cosmetic help of Bushy and Pancho, who watched with great interest and some critical input.

First I pulled my hair up into a severe topknot; then I wrapped my head in a Turkish towel, a turban of sorts. I was going to be a mad homeless woman.

I put on long johns, then a pair of ragged red denim pants. On my feet I put Tony's sweat socks and an old pair of his running shoes. They were much too big, of course, giving me a Chaplinesque air.

I found two old sweaters with holes in them

and put those on. And I wore all five mufflers I possessed, wrapping them around my face and neck, a kind of Eskimo homage.

I stared at myself in the mirror. I almost had it right—but not quite.

So I rouged my face heavily and then poured on the mascara, thick and dripping. Next I painted my mouth with a kind of fifth-generation Day-Glo lipstick.

Ready!

Except for a bag. A crazy homeless lady had to have an exceptional bag. It had to have the story of her life in it. It had to be large. It had to be memorable.

Back to the closet I went and dug out all the candidates. What an array. Backpacks. Suitcases on wheels and overnight bags with broken straps. Book bags. Laundry bags. Fraying shoulder bags from faraway places like Nepal and Barcelona.

There was one that looked especially bizarre. I chose that one, a carpetbag, an authentic old bag made out of a Persian rug. It was perfect. I stuffed it with fruit and old newspapers and books and anything else I could grab. Soon it was almost too heavy to lift. Yes, that was the way it was supposed to be. This was Method acting at its finest. This was verisimilitude.

I hoisted it and staggered a few feet.

"What do you think?" I asked the cats.

They regarded me skeptically.

"Yes, you're right. I need a good name."

I turned back to the mirror. Who should I be? Schizoid Sally? Ranting Rhoda? Wild Wilhelmina? Big Mamma Maybelle? Who?

"I've got it!" I cried in triumph. "Howling Hannah. How do you guys like it?" They seemed to approve, because they wandered off after that. I fed them well and left the apartment.

Of course, in my new role as Hannah, a hundred taxis refused to pick me up, so I ended up traveling to Sustenance House by subway.

It was almost time for the food line to form. There must have been twenty people waiting, in sedate single file, and probably ten more were being allowed to wait inside.

Demurely I took a place in line, lowering the tremendous weight of the carpetbag. In front of me was an old man with two canes. He turned to look at me once, a pained expression on his face, then never turned around again.

A younger man got on line just behind me and began to mutter over and over, "Are they serving yet?"

"Why don't you shut up for a minute and you'll see?" I responded testily.

"Do I know you from the West Side?" he asked, quite civil now.

So this was Howling Hannah's intro to homeless life. I thought I was carrying it off quite well. Anyway, the line was now moving. A man at the front of the line kept shouting incoherently, something about gravy, about the importance of gravy, how it didn't much matter what the hell they served in winter as long as the gravy was good and ample.

Then I was inside. The moment I stepped back into Sustenance House in another persona, I wondered whether I was committing some kind of crime.

I picked up a tray and shuffled along with the others. I could see several of the board of directors manning the stations—not all of them, but Devries and Jack and Raya Lambert were in evidence.

Another woman, with great wisps of unmanageable straw-colored hair, began to move along the back of the food line. She was carrying a tub of clean serving utensils, distributing them to the servers. She didn't have to wear a hat like the others because she wasn't dealing directly with the food.

This woman was my prey, I realized. This was Daisy. The minute she came into view I remembered her last name: Eidan. Daisy Eidan.

Now, I directed myself. Start your act.

I left the line, circled behind the people ahead of me, and peered over their shoulders at what was being served. "Beef stew?" I screamed out. "Is that what you're giving us? Beef stew! I thought you people had a big fat goose all the time."

They all stared at me tolerantly. Jack and David Devries and Raya and Daisy and all the hungry ones and the security people. All of them, looking at *me*. But none of them saw Alice Nestleton beneath Howling Hannah's getup.

It was Jack who said gently, "There is goose on Christmas Eve—maybe."

"No good, no good," I said disgustedly.

They all turned away from me then. I walked away from the food line, toward the back of the room.

"Where are you going, miss?" a security guard asked me.

"Where do you think I'm going, you fool? To the can."

"Leave the tray outside," he commanded.

I thrust the thing into his hands and continued my march to the ladies' room. But at the last minute I slipped through another door, the one that read STAIRS, and climbed swiftly to the second floor.

The floor was deserted. All the doors, five on each side of the hall, were closed. A piece of tape with a name stenciled in was on each door. I knew that the second and third floors of Sustenance House were used as residences for the homeless. And I knew that the floors were segregated by sex. But I did not know which was the women's floor and which for men.

I tried the first door I came to. It was unlocked. I smiled. Basillio had once told me that all halfway houses and charity facilities make it a rule never to lock anything. If someone is caught stealing, he or she is immediately booted out and forever banned from residence. I guess Tony knew what he was talking about, though I didn't know how he knew that.

I walked slowly down the hall reading the names on the doors. No Eidan here or on the other side.

Then I crept up to the third floor. The name Eidan was there—third door on the right from the stairs. I took a deep breath, opened the door, and slipped quickly inside, closing the door behind me.

I waited for several moments in the darkness, listening for noises within and without. All was quiet. I flicked the wall light on.

It was a very small and efficient living space. There was a narrow bed, one chair, a little desk with a radio, a small sink on one wall, a mini-refrigerator, a hot plate, and an unvarnished wooden wardrobe with a mirror on the back of its door.

The toilets and showers were obviously communal, located elsewhere on the floor.

I pulled off the stupid mufflers and the turban and got to work. I didn't know what I was looking for really except it had to be something that would confirm Mrs. Boyle's testimony: Daisy Eidan had participated in the murder of Frank Loeb. If in fact the "frizzled and frazzled" head the old woman had seen was Daisy's. I didn't see how it could be other than Daisy.

First the bed. I stripped it. I searched the mattress, the spring, the pillow, the linen. Nothing.

Then under the sink. Then the refrigerator. Nothing.

The small desk had three drawers. I removed them one at a time and dumped the contents on the bed. A few letters from New England. Packs of chewing gum. Old movie magazines. Pens and pencils fastened with rubber bands. A book of stamps. Nothing really.

I replaced the drawers and turned my attention to the wardrobe. At the bottom were her shoes, three or four pairs. Two of the pairs jangled when I picked them up. I peered inside; she had left tins of shoeshine polish there.

Then to the clothes rack. Three skirts. Two coats. A bathrobe and a nightgown. I searched each garment carefully. Again, nothing.

I moved on to the top shelf of the wardrobe. There were panties and slips on one side and towels and washcloths on the other. I stepped away from the plain wood cabinet.

Whatever this Daisy Eidan had been in the past, she was now living the most spartan of existences.

I closed the doors of the wardrobe. They wouldn't shut entirely. A pair of shoes, weighted by those shoe polish tins, had slipped down, blocking closure.

I bent down to push the shoes back. My eyes caught those shoe polish cans again. I realized something was peculiar.

I picked the tin out of the shoe. It was not polish. It was a can of Amoré Natural cat food.

All the cans in her shoes were cat food! I flung the cans onto the bed. What were these cans about? Had Tiny and Tim lived here? Was Daisy the one who had sent me the candy cane and directed me to the Barking Ark?

I sat down on the bed. I stacked the cans. I was going to wait for her, as long as it took. I turned out the light and waited.

Daisy returned to her room an hour and fifty minutes after I had entered. She flicked on the light, shut the door behind her, and saw me immediately. She did not appear to be frightened.

"What are you doing here?" she asked in a quiet voice.

"Daisy, do you know who I am?"

"Yes."

"But you didn't know when I was downstairs in my bag lady regalia?"

"What do you mean, when were you downstairs?"

In lieu of an answer I held up one of the cans.

She smiled. "Didn't you know the homeless eat a lot of gourmet cat food?"

"You sent me that candy cane, didn't you?"

"Yes."

"You dropped the cats off at the Barking Ark."

"Yes."

"You took them from Frank Loeb's apartment."

This time she did not confirm my statement. Her tongue flicked nervously out over her lips. I noticed there were several small burns on the inside of her arms—probably, I figured, from handling hot food vessels.

She took out a cigarette and lit it, saying, "There is no smoking in Sustenance House."

"I'm waiting," I said.

Still, she did not reply to my remark about Frank Loeb.

"Would you rather speak to the police, Daisy? You see, now there is an eyewitness who's placed you at the scene of the murder. She lives right next door to Frank Loeb's apartment."

"Murder!" she barked. "There was no murder. It was his own fault. He was in a rage. He attacked Jack on the landing. He tripped and fell down the stairs."

"Jack . . . Rugow?"

"Yes. Three of us went over there. David stayed downstairs in the car. Jack and I went upstairs. We knocked on Loeb's door, and he opened it. He told us to leave. Jack tried to reason with him. But Loeb became hysterical, crazy. He started to fight with Jack. Then he fell. We panicked and left. But I saw two lovely cats at the top of the landing. They were staring at Loeb's body. I felt awful about it. I couldn't just leave them there. I brought them here and kept them in my room. But David kept telling me to get rid of them. He wouldn't relent. So I dropped them at that pet store where people come to adopt pets. Then I wrote to you. After all, everyone said you were called the Cat Woman."

"Why did you go to Frank Loeb's apartment in the first place? Loeb was supposedly an anonymous donor. How did the three of you come to make this visit, and what was Jack trying to 'reason' with him about?"

I was shooting the questions out like bullets. My fury was growing, for now I realized how I had been manipulated: Both Devries and Rugow had known who their benefactor was before they enlisted my services. I was just cover, a way to maintain the fiction that they didn't know the identity of Sustenance House's generous guardian angel.

Daisy Eidan stared at the burning tip of her cigarette. The strange appearance of this woman lay not only in her bizarre hair but in her angularity. Her bones were sharp and pointed. There were no contours to her.

"You see," she said, "my chores here include outside shopping. Every day, at least once, I leave Sustenance House and go to the supermarket or the hardware store."

She put the cigarette out in the sink. She sat down on the bed beside me and looked straight ahead.

She continued. "About six months ago I began to notice a man watching me when I left. He was sitting across the street on the steps of one of the brownstones. I thought he was a neighbor. We began to wave to each other. Then we would chat for a while. He was a nice gentleman. Then he asked me to have a cup of coffee with him. I told him it would have to be a quick one. That was fine with him.

"So we began having coffee together a few times a week. He always wanted to know how things were going at Sustenance House. He told me we were a wonderful place. He told me that his name was Frank Loeb, that he lived uptown, and he wished there were a Sustenance House near him.

"Sometimes I talked about the trouble I had gotten into. Sometimes he talked about music. But mostly it was about the misery of the homeless.

"Then, about six weeks ago, he invited me to have lunch with him in a beautiful new restaurant on First Avenue. I accepted. It was a wonderful lunch. We were both drinking a lot. And laughing a lot.

"He started asking me questions about where Sustenance House gets the money for all its programs. I told him the truth. Some money from foundation grants, I said, some from private charities, and some from state and federal funds. And I told him how we are particularly blessed because of an anonymous donor who gives us $81,000 every year in blank money orders.

"Suddenly he reached across the table and grabbed my wrist so tightly that I screamed. 'Shut up and listen!' he says. 'Tell them you just had lunch with their anonymous donor. And tell them they'll never get another penny from me. Because they're a bunch of thieves. I give them *$91,000* a year, not eighty-one.' Then he let me go, flung some money on the table, and walked out."

Daisy Eidan walked over to the sink, let the water run, then drank from a small glass. She lit another cigarette.

Her astonishing tale had cleared up at least one of my festering questions. Mrs. Boyle admitted to giving me only half of the money she found in the flute case—that is, $45,500. Now it made sense. Half of $91,000 was $45,500.

Daisy continued. "So I went back home in a state of shock. I told David what had happened. He locked the door and said there were some things he was going to tell me, but first he swore me to secrecy. He admitted that he and Jack Rugow had skimmed $10,000 off the top each year. But David said he had done nothing dishonest with his part of the ten thousand. Five thousand had gone to a charity for children in Vietnam and Cambodia who were still being injured by land mines and unexploded bombs from the war. The other five thousand had gone to keep Jack's repertory company alive. Both worthy causes, David said. And he reiterated that he had done nothing criminal. Because the money orders had been sent in without specific instructions as to how the money should be allocated.

"I listened. I said nothing. The next day he called me into the office. Jack was there too. They had decided to visit Frank Loeb. It was easy to find him now. We knew his name. And we knew he lived uptown. Devries said I must go with them. They had to explain things to Loeb. They had to persuade him to make his contribution and not to abandon Sustenance House.

"So we went up there. And the visit ended in death. But it was *not* murder."

She sat back down on the bed beside me, playing absentmindedly with the cans of cat food.

"Are they well? Those cats?" she asked in a minute.

I did not answer. I was overwhelmed by her story. What was true? What was false? Had it really been an accident that killed Loeb? Was the skimming of ten thousand dollars a year really just a reallocation of funds and not criminal embezzlement?

I wondered what to do next.

Then I remembered what Detective Rothwax had told me many years ago. "Cat Woman," he said, "one day you'll come upon some important information and you simply won't know what to do with it. Don't panic. Just get into a cab and go downtown. To a place called the Manhattan district attorney's office. There are twenty-one hungry assistant DA's just waiting there for you. With a whole bunch of detectives to back them up. Just give them what you have. Believe me, they'll do the rest."

I slowly re-coiled the turban around my head and rewound all the mufflers about my neck.

"Are you leaving?" Daisy asked.

"We both are leaving. Now. Together. Arm in arm, right out of Sustenance House. Someone else wants to hear your story."

"Do I have a choice?"

"None."

She lit another cigarette. She took two puffs

and put it out in the sink. "Take the cat food," she said.

I put the cans in my already groaning bag. The two homeless women then exited the premises. Not an eyebrow was raised.

Chapter 10

'Twas the night before Christmas
And all through the place
Not a money order could be found
There was hardly a trace.

Yes. It was Christmas Eve.

Tony was back from New Haven, waiting for me with Tiny and Tim. He wanted to make love to me.

Nora was in her Pal Joey bistro, waiting for me. She wanted to share a bottle of champagne with me.

Pancho and Bushy were waiting for me in the loft. They wanted to chew on the Christmas tree I had promised to bring home.

And where was the elusive Alice Nestleton,

whom everyone was waiting for? Huddled under the Fifty-ninth Street bridge.

I had started out with a plan and a goal. Now, only two blocks from the goal—Sustenance House—the plan seemed to be crumbling.

I stared up at the bridge. Traffic was moving across it. Beautiful beads of light. Christmas Eve in Manhattan is eerily magical. Everything seems to move in slow motion. Everything seems to take place against a backdrop of muted light. Voices are low and far away.

A cold wind was blowing from the north. I was bundled up, cowering and miserable even in parka and boots. No longer Howling Hannah. I was clearly Alice Nestleton now.

And in my huge parka pockets were $45,500 worth of postal and bank money orders.

I leaned against the stone wall that was the base of one of the bridge's giant supports.

Why had I lost my will so close to the finish line? I had to focus on Frank Loeb yet again. He was the only important element in the equation.

The others? Forget them. There was no way to tell whether anyone would be indicted.

There was no way to tell whether Sustenance House would survive the revelations of skimming.

And no way to tell whether they would ever serve their famous goose dinners again on Christmas Eve.

I had to sweep all those considerations from my mind now like so many cobwebs. Frank Loeb was the whole game. He had lived a saintly life. He had given everything he had—anonymously, asking nothing in return.

Then, for reasons of his own, reasons I might never discover, he had to know the details of Sustenance House's good works. He wanted to see the fruits of his saintliness. Perhaps he was planning at last to come out and claim credit for his good deeds. I'd probably never know.

But then he found something he had never counted on: His gift had been corrupted. All these years someone had been stealing from the cookie jar.

He must have been in a terrible rage, prompting a visit from the Sustenance House people—three of them anyway.

And his rage got him killed and orphaned two extraordinary cats.

That was the gist of things.

I closed my eyes and shivered in the cold night air. I had never met Frank Loeb. But I could imagine him now, overhead, on the bridge, playing his flute to the vehicles moving slowly by. A kind of gentle Yuletide piper. The vision warmed me, and my resolve returned.

I walked the short distance to Sustenance House. The feeding line was enormous; it already snaked around the block.

I walked to the very end of the line and took my place there, behind a tall, gangly fellow with matted hair and beard. He was shivering like mad and blowing into his bare hands.

"Hello," I said to him.

He looked at me. One of his eyes was shut; it looked infected. The good one, though, was a clear, placid blue.

He stared down at my feet. Fancy boots, he seemed to be thinking. Too fancy for a soup line.

I wondered what tales this man had to tell. I wondered where he was born.

Then, without my being aware that I had reached into my pocket, I was suddenly grasping a money order. I folded it and pulled it out carefully. "Here," I said to the blue-eyed man. "Take this." And I thrust it out toward him. "It's a present from Frank . . . from someone who loves you. Merry Christmas."

He took it, opened the sheet, and stared uncomprehendingly at the dollar amount: seven hundred dollars. Then he closed his good eye and began to sway ever so slightly, as if overcome by what it could buy: a warm, clean room for a month, a new coat, an ocean of alcohol, a steak every night.

He looked deeply into my eyes but never opened his mouth.

I went down the line and gave each waiting stranger a present from Frank Loeb along with his Christmas greetings.

When there were no money orders left, I walked quickly to Pal Joey, drank a champagne toast with Nora, and then borrowed twenty bucks so that I could buy a tree.

After I had placed and trimmed the tree and watched my kits take their first little nibbles and rubs, I headed for Tony's apartment.

My energy level was higher than ever, even though I had spent the last several hours in the strangest kinds of behaviors. Maybe I had moved into the kind of "high" that compulsive gamblers are supposed to experience. Not when they win. Winning only depresses them, so the shrinks say, and Basillio seems to agree with that analysis. It is when they lose everything they have that they really feel the rush of joy.

Of course I had not gambled away the money. I had given it away. But I had denuded myself of every dime, hadn't I? Maybe that was why—it had to be why—I was feeling so good. I began to laugh out loud as my feet crunched on the dirty day-old snow. I had given away almost fifty thousand dollars!

It had been a long time since I had done something I knew—*knew*—was the right thing, knew beyond any shadow of a doubt. I had the sudden delicious thought that a legend would grow up around this mysterious Saint Alice of the Breadline. That she might show up any Christmas, anywhere in the world. And when she did, there would be seven hundred dollars for you . . . and for you . . . and for you and for everyone.

A block from Tony's place I woke from my fantasy world and wondered what I was supposed to bring. Then I remembered. He'd said he was preparing dinner with his own hands and he didn't need help of any kind or any advice. Oh, Lord, what was it going to be: Falafel? Fish sticks and ice cream cake? Or take-out hamburgers heavily laced with the dreaded pork sausage?

I climbed the stair empty-handed and knocked at his door. It took awhile for him to answer, and when he did, he was oddly subdued. I had expected, I must admit, a fevered rush to the door. After all, it had been awhile, and his behavior from afar had been filled with passion bordering on the insane.

All he did was give me a little smile and sweet hi. So I just gave him a peck on the cheek and walked past him into the apartment.

Tiny and Tim were in their usual spot. I bent down to greet the two of them, and they purred their hearts out. I could smell something good emanating from the kitchen. Something good and very exotic. My! Was Tony roasting a goose?

Then I heard him say: "We have a visitor."

"A wise man, no doubt," I quipped, straightening.

"Something like that."

For the first time I saw that his face was ashen and utterly without animation. He made a slight movement with his head as if to direct my gaze to the sofa.

I looked over that way. Jack Rugow was seated there, calmly staring at me.

"What are you doing here, Jack?" I demanded, unfriendly as hell.

He smiled. That was all. And I noticed that he still had his overcoat on and that his hands were folded demurely on his lap. Furthermore, an old linen table napkin of mine, one of the many things I'd left behind when I moved out of the apartment into my new place, was draped across his hands.

"I thought," Jack said, "it might be nice to eat here on Christmas Eve. And maybe on Christmas day too. That's something that's always confused me, Alice. In Western Europe, you know, when they talk about Christmas dinner, they mean the meal on Christmas day. But in the eastern part of Europe they are talking about Christmas Eve dinner."

Huh? What was he babbling about? What did I care about what time they ate dinner in Eastern Europe?

"Tony, do me a favor and get him out of here."

Rugow smiled again and said, "Besides, we're all theater people. Shouldn't we be among our own on this holiday? Shouldn't we look after each other and nurture each other? I mean, we carry a torch from generation to generation . . . I mean."

"Tony! Get him out of here, or I will."

"Shut up!" Rugow suddenly barked savagely, flipping the napkin off his lap and exposing the short 9mm automatic weapon he held in his left hand.

Fear broke out all over me.

Then his mood changed—if changed is the right word. For he turned on a dime. He was positively gentle now.

"I'm really here to bring you a kind of update, old friend Alice. Because I knew you'd want to know what's happening. After all, none of it would be happening if it weren't for you. Well, I never got to Sustenance House today because I received a phone call. Guess what? David Devries and I are going to be indicted for involuntary manslaughter in the death of Frank Loeb. What do you think of that, old friend?"

I didn't answer. I looked quickly at Tony. The look he returned was one of both fear and confusion. After all, Tony didn't know what had been going on with the case. He had no idea at all what Jack was talking about.

"Nothing to say, Alice?" Jack asked simperingly. "Why's that? I thought you'd be very happy to hear it because it was you who brought Daisy Eidan down to the DA's office, wasn't it? Who forced that poor woman to say what they wanted her to say? Well, maybe my other news will get more of a rise out of you. It also seems that David and I are being indicted on grand larceny charges for embezzling funds belonging to Sustenance House. Now, surely that's something to warm the cockles of your detecting little heart. Come on, Alice, can I see a smile from you?"

I said nothing. My face was immobile.

"What more could you possibly want?" asked Jack. "You got it all. It's all tumbling down. Isn't that what you wanted? When they send me away, the repertory company will fold. And when they put David away, Sustenance House will become just another dreary agency."

I finally was able to speak. "You were the one who brought me in on this. As a subterfuge. You have only yourself to blame, Jack. You and Devries used me. Don't you dare sit there and say it's otherwise."

"That is true. That is so true," he replied. "We really thought we were covering our tracks by bringing you in. We figured that if and when the police connected Frank Loeb to Sustenance House, there was no chance of tying us to his murder. We didn't know who he was—right? We'd even hired an investigator to find him and ask him to continue his donations."

He then laughed a long, unmerry laugh. It seemed to me he had crossed the line into psychosis, and that made the whole situation all the more worrying.

"Come, Alice," he said finally. "Sit down beside me. Keep me company in my hour of need. Even Humpty-Dumpty needs a friend."

"No," I said quietly.

He pointed the weapon at Tony. "Do what I tell you or I will put a bullet in your true love's head and then in each of his cats."

I walked slowly to the sofa and sat down as far from him as possible. The moment I sat down, Tiny jumped up onto the sofa between us and just sat there. I was petrified for a moment. Would he hurt the cat? But no, he seemed not to notice her at all.

"Now, let's have some Christmas cheer," Jack ordered. "What do you have to drink?"

"Wine," Basillio answered dully.

"No, not wine! No. We need something stronger than that, lover boy. This is more than just a Christmas celebration. It's an everything-has-tumbled-down party. It's a last stand."

"I have grappa," said Tony.

"Perfect, perfect. The brandy of the Italian working classes. Yes, pour us some of that. I hear that in the Italian Alps, when the floods come and the men are digging restraining walls from dawn to dusk, they start the day with grappa. It puts strength in their lungs and legs."

Tony brought the bottle and the glasses and placed them on the low coffee table beside the sofa.

"Pour," Jack commanded. Tony obeyed.

"Serve," Jack commanded. Tony obeyed.

We all drank, but none so greedily as Jack. And he kept on drinking.

After the third glass, he said, "Would you like to know what I really thought of you as an actress, Alice?"

The answer was no, but I didn't say anything.

"I mean, you do have this awesome underground kind of reputation, don't you? You're your own little one-woman cult. So how come, in all these years, I never offered you a good part with the Rep? I'll tell you. Because I don't care very much for your stuff. When you were young, there was too much Method. And as you got older, there was too much movement. No good, no good. I like actors with quiet bodies."

Apparently he found his own words very funny because he was laughing uproariously.

There was a movement on the sofa cushion just then. Tiny jumped down, and then Tim replaced her on the couch. I tensed again. How would he react?

But all he did was scratch the lady's neck gently, almost, it seemed, without thinking.

"I guess I might as well tell you both how I got into the theater in a big way . . . I mean, how the idea for a rep company came to me. Don't you want to know before dinner? Sure, you do. I was a starving young actor—familiar story, huh? A friend of mine got a job as a stagehand in that famous *Hamlet* on Broadway. The one with Gielgud and Burton and Hume Cronyn and a whole bunch of other fine actors. We used to meet afterward in one of those cafeterias on Broadway— Hector's, it was called—and my friend would tell Gielgud stories. Like how, after one performance he had said to Burton, 'You were brilliant tonight, Richard. I almost liked it.' Oh, I grew to love those stories. I couldn't get enough of them. And then he told me what Gielgud had said to John Cullum, who was the Laertes, after a performance one night: 'You are not moving correctly. You must not scurry. You must stride.' And for some reason that hit me in the head. You see, I too was scurrying. I had to learn to stride. To stride out. To stride forward in seven-league boots. That's when I got the idea of forming my own company."

He downed another shot of grappa, then screamed out: "Stride! You must stride!"

Immediately both cats leaped onto his lap. I flinched with fear. But he only moved the weapon away from them a bit.

Jack began to babble then, to sing and curse, with the weapon in his hand and the cats on his lap.

My legs began to cramp from the tension. Tony's eyes were riveted to Rugow's hand. I closed my eyes in helpless exasperation.

Little by little, Jack grew quieter. And then . . . silence.

I felt a pressure on my leg. When I opened my eyes, Basillio was standing beside me. He put his finger to his lips, cautioning silence. Then he pointed to Jack. Our captor was slumped against the arm of the sofa, saliva dribbling down his chin.

Tony pointed to the cats. He motioned to me to pick them up.

I slowly leaned over and scooped them up. Tony took a deep breath and bravely pulled the gun out of Jack's loosened grip.

We both leaped up then, waiting for a response. There was none. Jack Rugow was dead to the world, as my grandmother would have put it.

We tiptoed to the kitchen.

"He's not sleeping," Tony said. "He's unconscious. If you're not used to drinking that stuff in cold weather, it will put you away."

I headed for the phone. "I'll call 911."

"No, don't." Tony called me back. "Look." He was holding the clip from the weapon. "This thing isn't loaded. There are no bullets in the clip."

We sat down, exhausted, at the kitchen table, the unloaded gun between us on the tabletop. The idea of calling the police seemed foolish now. They would have him soon enough.

Tony reached across the table for my hand. "God bless grappa," he said.

But I knew in my heart that it wasn't the drink

that had finally disarmed Jack Rugow. "And God bless Tiny Tim," I added, "wherever they are."

It was Christmas morning. Early morning—freezing cold and still dark.

Tony was fast asleep beside me. I was back in the safety of my own home, but I had not slept well at all. No doubt the confrontation last night with Jack Rugow in Tony's apartment accounted for my restlessness. Or maybe it was the collective impact of the last few days. I was still on edge. I was still waiting for something I couldn't define. But the Sustenance House case had been closed, cleared up, to everyone's satisfaction—everyone, that is, except the dead.

Our Christmas day had been carefully planned weeks ago. We would go uptown to Nora's for a festive brunch, stopping off to feed Tiny and Tim on the way. Then we all would go into Central Park, whether or not it was snowing. After that a movie. And the day would end with a sumptuous Peking duck dinner in Chinatown.

As for the gifts, I was proud of all my selections. For Bushy a new comb and brush set so that he could be more beautiful than ever, vain feline that he is.

For Pancho there was one half pound of the finest saffron rice I could procure from the Indian grocer on Lexington Avenue.

For Tony there was the mother of all Swiss Army knives. It had so many appurtenances it was absolutely ridiculous. There were four knife blades of differing sizes and edges, three files, a scissor, a compass, a can opener, a corkscrew, a magnifying glass, and, for all I knew, a fax machine. Yes, he would like that.

For Nora I had gotten a nineteenth-century cookbook written by a frontier housewife on the Great Plains. There were all kinds of good buffalo tripe recipes in it.

I sat up suddenly at a stab of memory: my grandmother giving me a wondrous book one Christmas, and accepting my gift with great thanks, then kissing me on the top of my head and asking: "Now what kind of gift do you have for the child Jesus?"

My eyes flooded with tears. Quickly and silently I rose from bed.

The silhouette of the tree loomed large, making the dear little green thing seem a great deal taller than it really was. I walked over and touched one of the branches. My cats had been kind; they had chewed it only a tiny bit.

I could see Bushy curled up on his rug. Where was Panch?

Aha. There he was, seated on one of the window ledges, peering down onto the street. Obviously he was waiting for his enemies from the outside to try coming in; he had probably spent the night escaping from his enemies inside.

I sat down beside him and looked down at the single streetlight that illuminated nothing. No one was about. Nothing moving. All was silent.

"You're safe, honey," I whispered. "There's nobody there."

I knew from the way he bared his teeth and arched his spine that he did not believe me. I crossed my legs and waited for a few minutes.

"Panch, how long are you going to sit here?"

His ears pulled forward a bit. I swooped him up in my arms and hugged him to me. He reacted as if he'd taken one of those courses at the Y telling you what to do if you're accosted by a mugger: He went absolutely limp.

"Buddy," I told him as I stroked him, "I don't care if the world says you're just an ugly old alley cat with half a tail and a coat like Brillo. To me you're the Albert Finney of the cat world. You're beautiful." I kissed him quickly and, to his relief, put him back down. "Now what do you think of that?" I asked, still whispering so as not to disturb Tony.

He looked at me gravely, but not for long. He immediately resumed his watch.

Suddenly both Pancho and I spotted movement on the pavement. I leaned closer to the pane and peered down. Two homeless men, obviously drunk, were staggering up the middle of the street. Their coats were open, and they were either arguing or singing. One had a massive red muffler at his throat. The other one, who wore a thin raincoat and no hat at all but had newspapers wrapped around his legs, suddenly sat down right in the street.

His companion just stared at him.

The one on the ground pulled a bottle out from under his garment and offered it to red muffler, who took it and drank. I could tell, even from that distance, that it was a champagne bottle.

I scratched Pancho's neck. "They're not after you," I assured him.

Homeless alcoholics drinking champagne. An odd sight. Then the force and logic of what I was seeing hit me. Perhaps these two men had been at Sustenance House earlier, on the food line. Maybe they were just two of the hundred or so to whom I had given money.

Suddenly what I had done hit me like a ton of bricks. I had given hundreds of dollars, in some cases thousands, to men and women who hadn't seen that kind of cash in years, if ever.

What had they done with it? The alcoholics no doubt had gone and purchased more good whiskey than they had ever purchased in their lives.

That was bad. Very bad.

I cringed. But then a whole lot of other options flooded my mind.

What about the homeless women who had to sleep in dirty, cramped, dangerous shelters? With Frank Loeb's money orders they could march into the Hilton and buy three nights' worth of bliss. Room service and barrels and barrels of hot water and cable TV and crisp white sheets.

What about the young men who panhandled for cigarettes and fifty-cent frankfurters? They could walk into the nearest supermarket and buy all the T-bone steaks they wanted and all the fresh fruit they could eat—even hothouse strawberries.

As I thought of the options, and most of them were good, I felt a kind of giddiness, a sense of power that I had never experienced before. Sure, I had acted in plays that had moved audiences. But I had never changed a single person's material existence, even for a day.

Now, throughout the city, hundreds of poor souls were feasting and bingeing on the things they craved. The things might be bad for them . . . surely . . . but at least they had the freedom to choose. And it was Frank Loeb and Alice Nestleton and Mrs. Boyle who had given it to them.

I felt wild, happy, strong. I picked Pancho up again and carried him out into the center of the loft, whirling in a crazy kind of dance.

"What is going on?"

I stopped. Oh, my. I had awakened Tony. He was staring at me, dazed.

"We're dancing, Tony. Pancho and me. That's all. And there are two derelicts downstairs drinking a magnum of champagne. And by the way, all's right with the world."

I wondered again what Tony would say if he knew I had given away $45,500 in unsigned money orders.

"Dance a little quieter, will you?"

"Yes, my lord," I called out. "By all means, my lord, we shall dance like butterflies."

Tony's head hit the pillow, and in a few seconds he was snoring away.

I held Pancho close. But we didn't dance anymore. We were listening to the celebration going on in the street.

Don't miss your chance
to enter the mysterious world of
Alice Nestleton and her feline pals
in the next book of
Lydia Adamson's popular series

A CAT ON STAGE LEFT

Coming to you from Signet
in November 1999

It was one of those late-August afternoons in the city where everything becomes absolutely still except for the heat, which seems to move in noisy waves.

I was seated on a window ledge looking out over the street. Not a soul on the street. Bushy sat beside me, also staring down. Pancho was investigating the food dishes, particularly the one with his dry pebbles. He scorned them but kept returning to the dish again and again, as if he was investigating why he loathed them so much. My Pancho might be quite mad, but he is at heart an old gray intellectual.

Tony was fast asleep in my bed, having executed his usual behavior patterns: He showed up late last night, straight from a job at a summer theater near Cape May. We made love. Then I fed him. Then I went to sleep. He stayed up all night pacing. When I got up in the morning, he went to sleep, and he's been sleeping since.

The overhead fan was working fine, but nothing could cut through the heat. I sat and watched and sweated. What I was watching for I don't know.

Then the phone rang. I picked it up at the first ring, not wanting to wake Tony.

It was a woman's voice. "Are you Alice Nestleton the cat-sitter?"

I began to laugh. It seemed to be such a strange question. *Are you Alice Nestleton the cat-sitter?*

I mean, why not, "Are you Alice Nestleton the actress?"

Or Alice Nestleton the gingersnap cookie addict?

Or Alice Nestleton, of *the* Minnesota Nestletons?

Or Alice Nestleton, the lady with the strange paranoid cat with only half a tail who loves saffron rice?

Then I recovered. I said, "Yes, I am. Who is this?"

"My name is Mary Singer," the caller said.

She had a husky, jumpy voice. She stopped

talking after identifying herself, as if waiting for some kind of recognition from me.

But I didn't know her at all.

"Pernell Jacobs recommended you," she said in explanation.

Now *that* name rang a bell, but for the moment I couldn't remember why. Then I did remember and I blurted out, "But I haven't seen Pernell Jacobs in more than ten years."

In fact, it was closer to fifteen years. Pernell Jacobs had been in Tony Basillio's and my acting classes at the old Dramatic Workshop on 52nd Street in the 1970s. I might have bumped into him once or twice since then—in the early or mid-1980s. Pernell was a very handsome black man and a damn good actor. But he was a bit flaky, as they say.

"I haven't been in touch with Pernell in years," I told the caller. "How could he know I do cat-sitting these days?"

The caller didn't seen at all fazed by that question. She simply chose not to answer it.

Of course, there were any number of ways Pernell might have found out that I care for kitties between roles now. It could have simply been a matter of his running into an old colleague of ours who had more current information on my life.

"Will you take care of Dante for me?" she asked.

"Is that your cat?"

"Yes. He's big and sometimes a bit playful."

"Well, Mary," I said, "anything short of a Bengal tiger is acceptable. How long will you be away?"

"About four days."

"Starting when?"

"Starting now. When can I bring Dante over?"

"Oh, no. Just a minute. You don't bring the cat to me. I don't board cats. I'll come to your apartment while you're away and take care of him."

"That's not possible. Why can't you keep Dante with you?"

"Look. I told you. I don't run a boarding kennel. Why don't you just look in the Yellow Pages? You'll find one quick enough."

Mary Singer didn't respond. I waited. I hoped she would hang up forthwith.

Then I heard some garbled words.

"What? I can't hear you."

She said loud and clear: "I will pay you twenty-five hundred dollars to board Dante for four days."

"Twenty-five hundred!" I was incredulous.

"In cash. Up front. Just four days."

I didn't know how to respond. That was a lot of money to me at the time. A whole lot of money. But boarding? With Pancho and Bushy in the loft? Dangerous, very dangerous.

Again, she took my silence as an affirmation.

"I'll be in front of your apartment house in twenty minutes with Dante and the cash."

"It's not an apartment house. It's an old warehouse converted to lofts."

She hung up.

I looked around, growing increasingly frantic. What had I done?

What did I know about Dante? Nothing. Was he neutered? Was he hostile? How did I know there wouldn't be a battle royal? The only thing worse than a dog fight is a cat fight, because the kitties tend to hurt each other very quickly once they really engage.

Call her back, Alice, I told myself. Forget the twenty-five hundred. But I hadn't gotten her phone number. Was she in the phone book? Maybe. Maybe not.

I calmed down a bit. Tony was beginning to talk in his sleep.

What about a barrier? There were no doors in my loft except for the bathroom and the closets—and I surely couldn't keep Dante in one of those spaces for four days. But if I had some planks of wood, I could improvise a closed cat run in the loft.

If . . . if . . . if . . .

Pancho made a dash toward the bed but at the last moment veered off.

Bushy, my Maine coon cat, ambled under the beat-up dining room table and started to preen and groom himself. He was quite vain.

Then the solution came to me, right out of the air, as they say.

I simply would not take Dante out of his carrier. Tony would transport him immediately to his apartment—which used to be my apartment—and keep him there for four days, bringing him back to my loft just before Mary Singer arrived home to claim him. True, Tony had cats of his own now—two Siamese. But Tiny and Tim, as they were called, were so kind and sweet, you could put a hound dog in the room with them and not have to worry.

It was a wonderful solution. Everyone would be happy—with the possible exceptions of Tony and Dante. As for Tony, I'd give him half the twenty-five hundred to decrease his sadness. And as for Dante—well, maybe whole sardines and sweet cream and a lovely velvet mouse and some special organic cat grass and tea parties with the world's finest catnip.

Yes. It was a wonderful plan. I smiled as I watched Anthony Basillio sleep. Lover and friend and colleague. In what order? Should I wake him now and tell him, or wait until Dante was outside the loft in his carrier? I decided to postpone notification.

Then I walked out of the loft and downstairs to pick up the package.

The street was baking in the sun, but there was a surprisingly strong hot breeze whipping about. I leaned against the building.

Nobody was out—not even the dog walkers. Even the two winos from the east corner, who were permanent fixtures on the block, had sought shade and relief elsewhere.

I closed my eyes. Upstairs the heat was terrible. On the street, for some reason, it was bearable.

A car turned the corner and very slowly came down the street.

It was an astonishing vehicle. A wine-red Bentley with whitewall tires and all the chrome on it shined to a fare-thee-well. Was it chrome or was it sterling silver?

I stepped toward the curb. I didn't know cars like this still existed except on movie lots.

The car stopped. And out of the Bentley stepped a character even more unbelievable than the vehicle he was driving.

This was the dream chauffeur of all time. He was dressed in a luxurious gray uniform, and he must have been absolutely broiling in the heat.

He wore tall, brightly shined black-laced boots. Yes, laced high.

I was fascinated by his cap—the old-fashioned crushed kind with a small visor.

To make matters more bizarre, he was actually wearing some kind of driving goggles.

I couldn't tell whether he was thirty or sixty, but he was in excellent physical shape: erect, broad-shouldered, flat-stomached.

"Are you Miss Nestleton?" he asked.

"I thought I was. But now I'm not sure," I replied.

He didn't get the humor. He said gruffly, "Good!"

Then he opened the rear door. I could see a man on the far side of the seat. Next to him, closer to me, was a woman. And on the seat beside her, a carrier. It was one of the largest cat carriers I have ever seen. Inside the carrier I could make out two doleful eyes.

The woman—she was wearing a washed-out red dress and her hair was curly black—started to climb out of the Bentley with her cat.

Suddenly the man who had been sitting next to her gave her a violent shove.

Woman and carrier came hurtling out. The edge of the carrier smacked me on the knee.

I fell down.

I found myself on all fours, the pavement biting into my palms, staring at the woman who had been thrown from the car.

She, also, was on all fours. Her face was very lined—like Lotte Lenya at the end of her career.

"Are you okay?" I asked.

She didn't answer.

"Are you Mary Singer?"

Again, no answer.

A shadow fell over me. I looked up. The chauffeur. He had something in his hand. He pressed it against the back of the woman's head.

I didn't realize the object was a gun until he pulled the trigger.

The woman fell forward. Her face hit the pavement hard.

The chauffeur climbed into the car. The Bentley purred off.

For some reason all I could think of was Dante—the cat in the carrier. Help the cat, I said to myself. Save the cat.

My hands fumbled with the clasps. Wildly. My fingers were like trembling sticks. Finally I got the thing open and swung the top up.

Then I stared in disbelief at the large stuffed toy cat with painted buttons for eyes.